BIG ERNIE'S NEW HOME

A Story for Children Who Are Moving

by Teresa and Whitney Martin

MAGINATION PRESS • WASHINGTON, D.C.

Published by
MAGINATION PRESS®
An Educational Publishing Foundation Book
American Psychological Association
750 First Street, NE
Washington, DC 20002

Magination Press is a registered trademark of the American Psychological Association
For more information about our books, including a complete catalog, please write to us,
call 1-800-374-2721, or visit our website at www.maginationpress.com.

Printed by Phoenix Color, Hagerstown, MD

Library of Congress Cataloging-in-Publication Data

Martin, Teresa.
Big Ernie's new home : a story for children who are moving / by Teresa and Whitney Martin.
p. cm.
ISBN 1-59147-382-9 (hardcover : alk. paper) — ISBN 1-59147-383-7 (pbk. : alk. paper)
1. Moving, Household—Juvenile literature. I. Martin, Whitney, 1968- II. Title.
TX307.M38 2006
648'.9—dc22
2005027069

10 9 8 7 6 5

For our little movers
Roddy, Whitney, Ernie, Ella, and Pablo
All our love, Mommy and Daddy

In an old house, on a steep hill,
there once lived a very brave cat.
His name was Ernie.
Everyone called him Big Ernie.

Big Ernie lived with a little boy named Henry.
Every morning Little Henry made Big Ernie a delicious tuna breakfast.
And after breakfast, they always went for their morning adventure.
Even when it rained in winter.

Big Ernie was not scared of anything.
Not even flying dragons.

One time he even rode in a cable car.

Every afternoon,
after the fog disappeared,
Big Ernie curled up
in his favorite chair.
He drifted off to faraway places.

At night, when the streetlights started to hum,
Big Ernie liked to play with his best friend, Pablo.

After a game of cat and mouse, Big Ernie snuggled into his nighttime place.
He said goodnight to the cowboy riding into the sunset.
He said goodnight to the flying red dragon hanging on three strings.
And he said goodnight to Pablo, sleeping among Little Henry's things.

Big Ernie was very happy.

He was happy until one especially foggy morning,
when Little Henry said,
"We aren't taking a walk today, Big Ernie.
It's time to put our toys in boxes.
Today we're moving to a new home."

Boxes and boxes and more boxes
appeared everywhere Big Ernie went.
"It's time to stop playing," said Little Henry.
"It's time to put Pablo in a box.
Don't worry. He'll be okay."

Little Henry picked up Big Ernie and said, "It's time for us to say goodbye now."
"Goodbye ocean waves. Goodbye trees. Goodbye cable cars.
Goodbye bridge. Goodbye streetlight. And goodbye house."

After saying goodbye, Big Ernie saw IT.

THE RED BOX.

The red box meant only one thing.

Dr. Shep's office.

OH, NO!

"Oh, Ernie," said Little Henry,

"we're not going to the doctor's office.

This is a different kind of trip.

Today we're moving to our new home."

The car passed by the doctor's office.

Big Ernie meowed loudly,

"Where are we going?

What's a 'new home'?"

When the car door finally opened, Big Ernie knew he was in a new place.

He couldn't feel the rain and fog against his whiskers.

He couldn't smell the dinner rolls baking at Wong's.

He couldn't hear the bells ringing on the cable cars.

All he could hear was the whisper of the wind on his fur.

Ernie was a little worried. He wasn't feeling so "Big" in this new place.

Little Henry crouched down by Big Ernie. He said, "There are a lot of wonderful things to see and do here. Let's start with one of our favorites, a tuna breakfast."

Big Ernie needed to eat a lot of tuna breakfasts before feeling big enough to take his morning adventure. Then one day, after an especially delicious meal, Little Henry and Big Ernie stepped outside their door. SLOOOWLY. VEERRRY SLOOOWLY.

"Big Ernie, say hello to Santa Fe. This is our new home," announced Little Henry.

NEW HOME? How could this be home?
The colors were all wrong. Everything was brown and white.
Where were the red dragons? Big green trees? Blue ocean waves?
Everything smelled like chili. Where was the wonderful smell of fish?
And everything felt different, too. There wasn't even a sidewalk.
Big Ernie didn't like the cold, wet snow on his paws.

This couldn't be home.

Big Ernie was mad, and a little sad.
He had trouble sleeping.
He meowed all day and paced around the house.
Sometimes he even got into the red box,
hoping it would take him back to his old house.

Little Henry held Big Ernie tightly and said, "Ernie, I know you've been a little worried about living somewhere new. But you're still the Big Ernie. Even here."

Every morning, Little Henry brought Big Ernie his favorite tuna breakfast.
After their meal, Little Henry would take Big Ernie outside for their morning walk.
Every afternoon, Little Henry helped Big Ernie curl up on his favorite chair for a nap.
And every evening, Little Henry tucked Big Ernie into his nighttime place.

Little by little, Big Ernie started to look,
really look, around his new home.
At first all he could see was the brown and white.
But then he began to see adventures all around him.

He saw a familiar dragon peeking out from under an old cable car.
Maybe they have dragons and cable cars in Santa Fe, too.

Big Ernie smelled big-eared rabbits. They were playing cat
and mouse in the snow. Maybe they would let him play, too.

He heard the sweet music of water running.
The river wasn't big, but it did have a bridge to look over!

Big Ernie began to feel better.

When the sun went down,
Big Ernie snuggled up next to Little Henry in his nighttime place.
He said goodnight to the cowboy riding into the sunset.
He said goodnight to his flying red dragon hanging on three strings.
And he said goodnight to Pablo, sleeping among Little Henry's things.

The next morning, Big Ernie was waiting
to start their morning adventure.
He was ready for anything.
Even a new home.

Note to Parents
by Jane Annunziata, Psy.D.

Moving is a very big deal for kids. It's especially hard for younger children who haven't developed the cognitive and emotional resources to cope. Even a short move around the corner requires a lot of adjustment, but the more new things a child must adapt to, the greater the stress. Moves that are farther away are harder, since everything in the child's physical world — parks, preschool, grocery store — changes. A move to a different climate (such as Florida to Minnesota) or a different setting (city, suburbs, small town, or rural) also presents extra challenges.

The Child's View

Young children haven't had life experiences to prepare them for these changes. With less knowledge to draw from or plug in to, they react more than older children or adults might.

Also, because they are less intellectually developed, they rely more on their senses to process the world around them, and so are more sensitive to changes in sights, smells, sounds, light, and temperature. Even the water can taste different. The more sensory changes involved in the move, the more jarring it will be.

It's important for parents to remember that even when they view the move as positive, their child rarely does. A bigger or nicer home, a room of his own, a bigger backyard, more playmates, a parent who is home more because of a reduced commute—these things seldom override the feelings of stress and loss. Young children are very attached to the places and people in their lives. With this degree of attachment come corresponding feelings of loss when the attachments are disrupted, regardless of the compensations.

Finally, young children have trouble grasping the notion of permanence. No matter how well a move may be explained, they are likely to ask when they are going back to their old house. Over time, children mature cognitively and realize what it means for something to be permanent. They also put down roots in their new surroundings and slowly develop feelings of attachment. The good news, then, is that children eventually come to accept their new house as their home.

Explaining the Move

Before giving your child the news, let her know that you have something important to talk about. This allows her to be more emotionally prepared. If yours is a two-parent household, both parents should share the news, as this sends the message that everyone is in it together.

Keep your explanation simple, clear, and geared to your child's level of understanding. You could start with: "We have something important to talk to you about. There's a change coming up in our family. Mom is going to have a new job, and we are going to move to a new house near her new job. We know this will be a big change, even for Skipper! But we're excited about it too."

Address any of your child's questions or reactions, and in later conversations, slowly provide more and more age-appropriate information. Follow your child's lead in deciding how much detail to give and when.

Timing the News

The timing of the news is as important as how you relay it. The goal is to provide ample time for your child to prepare emotionally, while not telling so far in advance that the waiting seems to go on forever, creating more time to worry about it. For many preschoolers, two months is a good guideline, but consider your own child's needs. Children who have trouble transitioning will need more time than those who transition easily.

Make the time frame as concrete as possible by anchoring the move to things kids can understand, such as weather or holidays.

You might say, "It's spring now and the weather is just starting to get warm. We'll be moving at the beginning of summer, when it's really warm outside and we can go swimming and wear our shorts."

Anything else you can do to make it more concrete will help. Many preschoolers are familiar with calendars, for example. Your child can draw a circle around Moving Day and cross off the days or apply stickers as days pass. This will help him feel more in control of this very out-of-control life experience.

Reactions and Feelings

Be sure that children are given permission to have and express their full range of "moving" feelings—even the negative ones. When parents listen and help their children label and understand their feelings, the child is better able to navigate through them. Here are some common feelings that children experience:

- Loss. So many losses come with moving: house, bedroom, preschool, daycare, and more.
- Loss of control. Kids feel a total loss of control, expressed as: "No one asked me if I wanted to move!"
- Sadness. Grief is related to all of the loss involved in moving.
- Anxiety. This is a normal reaction to uncertainty.
- Anger. Anger results from all of the losses. Also, it can be an unconscious mask; the child stays busy with anger to keep the more upsetting feelings of sadness and anxiety at bay.

- Regression. Whining, backsliding in toileting habits, baby talk, and being oppositional are all normal reactions.
- Excitement! Last but not least, when kids are well prepared, they can feel some excitement about the things they do have to look forward to.

Reducing Stress

Parents can do many things to help their children adjust. If they seem to be having unusual difficulty with feelings of sadness or anger, do consult with your child's pediatrician or a mental health professional. In general, though, here are a number of things that parents can do to ease the process for everyone.

To begin with, introduce children to their new house and neighborhood before the move. If distance doesn't allow for that, show them pictures.

Create a gradual entry. Walk around the new preschool or daycare center before your child starts attending. Slowly familiarize him with the places and people he'll be getting to know.

As much as possible, keep the same things and routines in the new home: the same furnishings, the same activities, the same schedule.

Label regressive behavior and wonder aloud with your child about its connection to the move: "Maybe you're having a hard time using your four-year-old voice because you're upset about moving. Let's talk about what's bothering you, and you can make a picture of your feelings. I think that will help."

Help your child get involved in her new community by finding one or two activities outside of daycare or preschool

that she enjoyed in her old setting.

Give your child as much control as possible. Make sure he gets some say in the decoration of his room, the play equipment in the yard, and so forth.

Help your child keep her connections to people. Send a picture she makes, a photo, or a note or email that she dictates to you to an old babysitter, friend, or teacher. This will help her be more open to new people.

Help your child make a scrapbook with photos of his old home, room, and neighborhood. Include captions (and feelings!) that your child dictates to you. This is a helpful emotional outlet.

Enthusiasm is contagious. Communicate your own excitement!

Adjusting to a new home is a process that takes time, sometimes a full year or more. Reassure your children — and yourselves! — that this getting-to-know-you stage is normal. Some days will be better than others. Lend your children your optimism when they seem a little discouraged. Always acknowledge their feelings of loss, anger, and worry, but end your talks in a positive way. Your children will take their cues from you.

JANE ANNUNZIATA, PSY.D., is a clinical psychologist with a private practice for children and families in McLean, Virginia. She is also the author of many books and articles addressing the concerns of children and their parents.

Teresa and Whitney Martin
have recently survived moving to Santa Fe
with their two boys, two cats, and puppy.
This is their first book together,
after seventeen years of talking about it.

101
ANSWERS
TO QUESTIONS LEADERS ASK

QUINT STUDER

AUTHOR OF
HARDWIRING EXCELLENCE

101 Answers to Questions Leaders Ask
©2005 by Studer Group, LLC.
All rights reserved.

ISBN: 0-9749986-2-1

Library of Congress Control Number: 2005920657

Published By:
Fire Starter Publishing
913 Gulf Breeze Parkway, Suite 6
Gulf Breeze, FL 32561

12 11 10 09 08 07   4 5 6 7 8 9 10 11 12

"*101 Answers* is one of the most useful resources published today on effective hospital management. As health care leaders, we want to do what is right and good, but Quint Studer explains how to turn these intentions into daily actions that get results. Like other profound works, it seems deceptively simple, but in practice, will change the world."

> Steve Ronstrom, CEO
> Sacred Heart Hospital
> Eau Claire, WI

"Finally! A book that shows how to make common sense more common. I recommend that all health care CEOs get 'Studerized' for effective leadership in today's complex operating environment. Quint Studer is to health care management what Jack Welch has been to business management."

> Kent H. Wallace, President & CEO
> Baptist Health System
> San Antonio, TX

"Those leading change in health care share amazing commonality in the challenges before us. *101 Answers* is the indispensable resource we need to anticipate and respond to the nagging questions, perplexing situations, and inevitable obstacles that arise when any organization strives to move from good to great."

> Stephen Beeson, M.D.
> Sharp Rees-Stealy Medical Group
> San Diego, CA

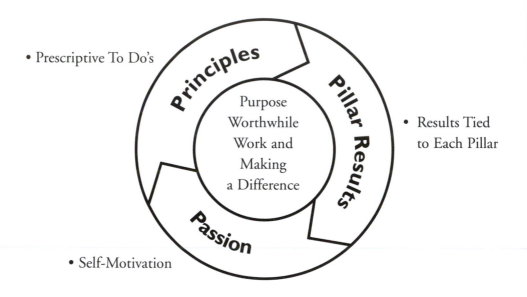

- Prescriptive To Do's

Purpose Worthwhile Work and Making a Difference

- Results Tied to Each Pillar

- Self-Motivation

Healthcare Flywheel[SM]

The Healthcare Flywheel demonstrates how self-motivation creates commitment to prescriptive actions that drive results in the Five Pillars of People, Service, Quality, Finance, and Growth. My hope is that this book turns the flywheel faster in your organization over the coming year.

Table of Contents

Chapter 5
Why Is Measuring Results So Important?............115

Chapter 6
How Can I Raise Patient Satisfaction? 127

Acknowledgments

First, I'd like to express my appreciation to the many organizations in Studer Group's national learning lab that are dedicated to the journey of making health care a better place for employees to work, physicians to practice, and patients to receive care.

I'd also very much like to thank the hundreds of individuals who contact me daily with these questions via the "Ask Quint" feature on our website. We find the good always want to get better. Thank you.

A special thanks also to Studer Group's many Coaches who freely share their expertise in answering these questions directly or helping me to do so.

And finally, I'd like to thank members of the review panel (Kimberly Carli, Lucy Crouch, Edward M. Goldberg, Mitch Hagins, Alexander W. Hiam, Maggie Ozan, and Margaret Pearce) who took time to read this manuscript and provide detailed suggestions on how to make this book more helpful. Your feedback is much appreciated.

Introduction

A Word from Quint Studer

I remember once hearing a line in an old country song, "I wish that I knew then the things that I know now." And that line certainly captures my own experience as a leader. When I look back over my career, how I wish I would have handled some situations differently!

I suspect that new leaders aren't always sure where to turn for information. And I know that even mature leaders benefit from talking with others about how to handle tough situations.

Fortunately, today in health care, an ever-increasing number of organizations are committed to providing consistent, focused training and educational resources to create, develop, and sustain great leaders. I hope *101 Answers to Questions Leaders Ask* will be one of them.

And as a last note, if you have a question that is not answered here, please e-mail me at quint@studergroup.com.

CHAPTER 1

HOW CAN I BETTER EVALUATE THE PERFORMANCE OF MY EMPLOYEES?

Our goal as leaders is to create a culture of ownership for attitudes, actions, and behaviors among employees. And for that to occur, individual accountability must be non-negotiable in any organization. When actions and behaviors are aligned with an organization's mission and values, we create a great place for employees to work, physicians to practice, and patients to receive care.

1. What are high, middle, and low performer conversations?

Question

What are high, middle, and low performer conversations? I am trying to engage staff and find myself always focusing on the low performers without much success. I also worry about the fairness issue. I don't want to be seen as playing favorites with my good staff.

Answer

In high, middle, and low performer conversations, your goal is to have key one-on-one conversations that move employees to the next level. By doing so, you can:

- Recognize and retain your high performers.
- Recognize and develop skills for your middle performers.
- Confront low performers, outlining specific steps to improvement so they understand it's "up or out."

Here are three sample conversation openers you might use for individuals in each of these categories:

High Performer: "Elvira, I just want to take this time to tell you how much I appreciate your support by coming in early, staying late, and being flexible in learning new tasks. I really appreciate having you here at Caring Heart Hospital."

Middle Performer: "Sandy, I want to thank you for doing an excellent job of responding to any question or task that I provide to you, but I would really like to see you develop some independence this next year and take additional initiative in the area of responding to patient concern letters."

Low Performer: "Becky, I know that you have told me that you are rounding on your staff, but when I talk to them they indicate that they don't see you. When you were hired, you agreed to meet our expectation to achieve patient satisfaction in your department at the 50th percentile, but you have not yet achieved this level."

Fact: The majority of leaders say that they spend 80 percent of their time on the small percentage of their staff who are low performers. High, middle, and low performer conversations reverse that percentage by having the leader focus first on high performers, then middle performers, and finally on low performers.

And on a final note, if you keep focusing on low performers without success, you need to make sure the low performers leave the organization. It's not fair for other staff, patients, and physicians to have to work with, or be cared for by, these individuals.

2. How do you sequence the high, middle, and low performer conversations at the leader level?

Question

Does the CEO meet with his senior leadership starting with the highs, then the middles, and finally the lows? And if you have a low performer in the senior group, who then meets with those high directors who report to this low performer? We are struggling a bit with the process.

Answer

In any case where a senior leader or director is considered a low performer, action needs to be taken quickly because of the impact that person has on his department. As part of the CEO's conversation with a low performer at the director level, the CEO might express a desire to work with that director by better understanding what the leader will be sharing during his high, middle, and low performer conversations with staff. In fact, one of the reasons the director could be a low performer is because he is not proficient at coaching his staff. You can also make sure you re-recruit high and middle performers who report to that leader. But again, the key action is to make sure that the senior leader improves or moves on.

3.

Do you use technical ability in classifying high, middle, and low performers?

Question

When classifying employees into the three categories for high, middle, and low performance, do you include an employee's technical ability with the evaluation or just her overall attitude, willingness to be a team player, etc.?

Answer

You include the total package. If an employee has a great attitude but cannot perform job functions, he or she is a low performer. If an employee has a lousy attitude and is a lousy team player, but is technically strong, he or she is also a low performer.

When re-recruiting high performers, what if certain departments don't agree on ratings?

Question

I am working with our CEO and VP of Human Resources on in-servicing and implementing high, middle, and low performer conversations (see Question 1) with our officers and directors group. One of the concerns expressed in our planning meeting centered on this question: "What if an immediate supervisor views a direct report as a high performer, yet the employees that person leads view him as a low performer?" We would like to work through that scenario prior to following through with the in-service. Any input/feedback would be appreciated.

Answer

Ultimately, I believe the dialogue must occur between leaders. Prior to doing the re-recruiting exercise, have each leader develop and turn in a list of the staff they view as high, middle, and low performers. Have your Senior Leader Team review this list and agree on ratings as they are defined by your organization. I don't feel that there will be discrepancies between a high, middle, and low performer rating if this occurs. Then, by having one-on-one meetings with high, middle, and low performers, you will be able to address three key drivers for satisfaction simultaneously: recognition and career direction for high performers, recognition and skill development for middle performers, and creating consistency with employees by addressing low performers.

Do excessive unplanned absences make an employee a low performer?

Question

If an associate has most of his or her performing criteria fall under the high performer category, but does not come to work on time and has an excess number of unplanned absences, does that make him or her a low performer? Can someone be in both categories?

Answer

I would say if an employee has excessive unplanned absences and does not come to work on time (unsure of frequency), he or she should be disciplined according to the guidelines of the organization. Even if the employee does a good job when he or she is there, I would classify him or her as a low performer due to the negative impact the absences and tardiness have on others. This person is not following work rules.

When you counsel employees with high absenteeism, explain that while you appreciate their work when present, the hospital provides care 365 days a year and their coworkers and patients depend on them 365 days a year. Therefore, individuals with similar excellent performance who have a better attendance record are more valuable to the organization. I find it is better to focus on their value to the organization instead of questioning whether their illness/absence was legitimate or not.

How do I deal with a staff member who thrives on gossip?

Question

I have been a pediatric nurse for a long time and I manage a children's practice. I have excellent employees, but there is one who thrives on gossip. What can I do? I asked that person to be a leader, and to refuse to participate in any gossip she hears. My approach hasn't worked, and I need your advice.

Answer

Here are my suggestions:

- If your organization has standards of behavior, I would guess gossip does not fit in. When she indulges in gossip, point out her mistake. If her behavior continues, handle it like you would any performance counseling.
- Have staff create a "What Is In/What Is Out" list. I would guess that gossip would be "Out." Once again point out the problematic behavior and handle it as a performance issue.
- Have those high, middle, and low performer conversations, and when you meet with this person, spotlight gossip. The conversations will move others to a higher level, so they won't be swayed by the gossiper.
- Finally, if this leader cannot stop gossiping after you have taken these steps, refer her to an employee assistance program.

Deal with this issue as a performance issue. And as with other performance issues that cannot be resolved, terminate the employee who refuses to change this behavior.

7.

How can one employee confront another one on behavior?

Question

I have an employee who is always talking about her peers negatively and the staff is exhausted by it. They are afraid to confront her, fearing that she will become even more difficult to work with. What is the appropriate way to approach this customer service issue?

Answer

This is not a customer service issue. It is a leadership issue. The coworker sounds as if she is a low performer. It is the leader's role to meet with her and discuss her performance. In fact, employees may be reluctant to confront a coworker because they fear the leader won't support them or action will not be taken. We recommend that leaders identify their high, middle, and low performers and confirm their judgments with the Senior Team. Then the leader can meet with individuals in each group.

High performers need to be re-recruited. Middle performers need to be supported and coached until they become high performers. We advise what we call a DESK technique with low performers:

D - Describe their current performance.

E - Evaluate their performance and share that you are disappointed with it.

S - Show the employees what is expected of them.

K - Know (share) the consequences of not improving performance. Follow-through is key to success.

Low performers need to know their behavior will not be allowed to undermine the team or the mission. This technique can work with any disruptive behavior and will be even more supported if the behavior is clearly not part of the standards of behavior.

What if an informal leader isn't on board?

Question

What is the best way to deal with "informal leaders" in a work group who are continuously negative, especially regarding "upper management"? These are the same people who will write letters and send petitions to the top leaders in the organization when they do not get the answers they want from their immediate supervisors.

Answer

I believe that "informal leaders"—often individuals who allegedly "represent" others' concerns but have no official job title to do so—succeed because formal leaders give them this power. My suggestion is to always inform high and middle performers about information first. In essence, freeze out the low performers with isolation. Also do not allow anyone to identify concerns by using words like "people," "staff," "anonymous," or other such vague words.

People can speak only for themselves, which is why anonymous letters or unsigned petitions should be thrown away. (The exception: if an ethical issue is raised, address it.) Same with petitions. If the petition has no name, then throw it away. As morale keeps improving, negative individuals will stand out more and more, creating pressure to get on board or leave the organization.

CHAPTER 2

HOW CAN I—AND WHY SHOULD I— HARDWIRE THE MUST HAVES^{SM} IN MY ORGANIZATION?

Studer Group developed its Must Haves to help focus organizations and leaders on actions that have the biggest impact on creating a Culture of Service and Operational Excellence. They are: Rounding for Outcomes, Employee Thank You Notes, Employee Selection and Early Retention, Discharge Phone Calls, Key Words at Key Times, and Leadership Evaluations.

The Must Haves are identified best practices that standardize leadership behaviors. Consistent execution leads to better patient outcomes and operating efficiencies. Hardwire the Must Haves and you will reduce employee turnover, raise patient satisfaction, serve more patients, increase quality, enjoy strong financial performance, and increase capacity.

How can we turn the Healthcare Flywheel^SM faster?

Question

What are we doing wrong? We are rounding. We are having focus group meetings. We are desperately trying to make improvements and changes. We have been at this for a year now. Employees are *still* negative and are talking to us less and less. Physicians feel we are being too hard on the employees at times. Any advice?

Answer

First, make sure all leaders are consistently Rounding for Outcomes on staff. Consistency will send a message to leaders that rounding on staff is a priority.

Make sure managers have been specifically trained to round on employees. At Studer Group, we find that productive rounding occurs when managers ask five questions:

- The first question is personal, to establish an emotional bank account (i.e., "Did you have an enjoyable vacation?" "Is your daughter over her illness?").
- The second is: "What's going right?" (to establish a positive climate).
- The third is: "Who else should I be rewarding and recognizing?" (which encourages staff to manage up).
- The fourth is: "What systems and tools can be improved?"
- The fifth is: "Do you have the tools and equipment to do your job?"

Using these key phrases will assure that you are Rounding for Outcomes.

Then follow up by responding to needs and capturing wins, making sure employees know that they have been heard. I have found that it's rare for all employees to feel one way or the other. Try to drill down to individuals. Look at the negativity by unit leaders and managers—often, it's the result of a lack of talent or skill set on the part of the supervisor. Sometimes, people are just negative by nature. The unsatisfied 5 percent can be, and usually are, the most vocal in attempting to derail the process. Avoid using generalities. If a leader says her staff is not responding to rounding, round with her again to make sure she is indeed Rounding for Outcomes as outlined above and is focusing on the positive staff first.

I might also suggest doing a mini employee survey to see if you can identify pockets of negativity. You will find that some unit leaders perform better than others. Learn from the high performers. Not all leaders are the same.

10.

What's the best way to ensure unit managers are rounding?

Question

Our unit managers are resisting our attempt to hardwire rounding. The resistance may be linked to our requirement that each manager "track" his or her rounding. Is it important to track rounding—i.e., to have managers report where and when they are rounding and pinpoint any unsolved problems? Or, is it sufficient to rely on the various bosses to ensure that their direct reports are rounding?

Answer

Organizations that use rounding logs outperform those that don't. Rounding logs are reviewed by appropriate VPs. Many times, it's the way the rounding log is presented that makes it most effective. The key is to present the rounding log by explaining what it will accomplish. Rounding logs serve many purposes. They:

1. Capture systems that are working well, so you can sustain results.
2. Highlight individual staff and physicians so they can be both complimented by supervisors and managed up to senior leaders.
3. Identify systems needing improvement and identify tool and equipment needs.
4. Help the organization identify chronic issues that have been missed.
5. Provide information for consistent reward and recognition. We also find that what gets documented in health care gets done. If rounding doesn't get documented, it will fall behind those things that do.

I would also encourage feedback from your managers. Determine what rounding log format works for them. Based on trial uses, what enhancements do they want to make?

In summary, I encourage you to read my article titled "Leader Standardization and Repetition" on the Studer Group website. You can find it at www.studergroup.com if you search on "standardization." It covers the need for hardwiring and explains why some managers push back. You are on the right track and can help turn the flywheel in your organization by encouraging leaders to use rounding logs. (You can also download a General Leader Rounding Log at the Studer Group website.)

11.

How do we implement senior leader rounding?

Question

We have hardwired nurse manager and department manager rounding and are ready to take the next step to implement senior leader rounding. Any advice?

Answer

If department leader rounding is hardwired, you are definitely ready for senior leader rounding. Just follow the nine steps below:

1. Identify someone in senior leadership to champion this effort. (The CEO is the best person you can choose.)

2. Develop a plan that includes a quarterly schedule for your senior leaders. It is key that they have a unit to round on once per week.

3. Develop your tools, including an e-mail template that senior leaders send to the manager before they round so they are briefed and can manage up the supervisor. This alignment is key to showing teamwork.

4. Present a plan and train senior leaders and their assistants on how to implement it. I highly recommend using Studer Group's Must Haves℠ video on senior leader rounding to do this.

5. Train leaders on the plan and explain why you are doing this (to support them!) and what you need from them prior to rounding. It is all about alignment of senior leaders and managers/supervisors.

6. Implement. The key is for senior leaders to do simple follow-up with managers in person or via e-mail.

7. Pick one day of the week for senior leaders to connect for 15 minutes to discuss the results of rounding.

8. Don't be shy—tell your staff what you are doing. Write an article about rounding that explains the challenges senior leaders face and how helpful it is for them to learn what's working and what needs to be addressed by talking with staff. You can also interview employees and ask if they like senior leader rounding.

9. And last, leave "evidence" that senior leaders have rounded. I find that no matter how well senior leaders round, some staff will say they never see them. Leaving evidence allows the leader to be visible to all. One CNO I know leaves a handwritten note to staff on the department's communication board with positive patient comments she read on patient surveys from the area she rounded on. When staff read it, they know she was there.

12.

How can we take senior leader rounding to the next level?

Question

I want to do senior leader rounding more often but have always felt uncomfortable about it. I feel I'm intruding on staff who may be very busy dealing with patients, etc. Could you help me with key words or any other tips?

Answer

First, hold your department leaders accountable for scheduling you. Once the schedule is set, many organizations distribute it so staff are aware of when senior leaders will be rounding in their area.

The purpose of senior leader rounding is to support the middle manager. Ask department leaders for a scouting report before you round in their areas. A scouting report for senior leaders is an e-mail or report that provides senior leaders with information about the department, including wins, new employees to welcome, staff to be recognized, new equipment, and so forth. It also highlights any issues that may come up. If a scouting report identifies a hot issue, then ask managers how they are handling it. This also helps you learn more about the skill sets of leaders. The scouting report ensures that the senior leader and middle manager are in alignment.

If a department has new equipment, tools, or systems, ask how they are working. Have a leader give you some people to compliment and when doing so, say, "Bob has told me how you came in last Saturday and helped out when we got so busy. Thank you." I suggest you put some ownership on leaders to provide you with any other items.

Walk with your leader, not alone. Ask what is working well. Ask what systems could be improved. Find out about birthdays, anniversaries, and so forth. In essence, go in with a plan and "talking points."

Attending staff meetings is good if an administrative update is included on the agenda. The key is to let unit leaders handle issues, so senior leaders are supporting and not creating a we/they situation. I believe senior leaders should attend area supervisors' meetings for at least a brief time, especially to manage up wins and recognize identified high performers. Attending staff meetings is not a substitute for rounding, however. Rounding on the units shows alignment with middle management.

13.

How do we overcome resistance to senior leader rounding?

Question

For months we have been rounding on a weekly basis with our senior leaders, and response seems to be regressing. People were positive at first. Now I am hearing comments from staff that it is insincere and that we are doing it only because we are required to. Should we cut back on rounding? Should we go to a bi-weekly schedule?

Answer

First, put criticism in perspective. I find health care leaders tend to weigh criticism much more than the positives they hear. Also, identify those who are complaining. Dig for specifics. You may have 5 percent of staff who are speaking as if they represent the majority. Often, the complainers are the low performers. They are hoping to back you down. Instead, move forward. Here are some of my general suggestions:

Continue rounding. Personally, I would increase my efforts. You will improve with practice. I find the more you round, the less staff find to complain about.

Spotlight and compliment people, while isolating negative people. Use the Gap Exercise of high, middle, and low performers. For detailed steps see *Hardwiring Excellence*, Chapter 6.

As for rounding because "you have to," keep in mind that we do most things in health care because we "have to." Either ignore people making this comment, or say something like, "Don't you want me to know how good you are to our patients and your coworkers?" Go on the offensive, instead of being defensive. If you really want to go on the offensive, try: "What don't you want me to see?"

Share the rounding schedule and the results from rounding. "Connect the dots" for employees on actions you are taking as a result of rounding. Show the staff the wins.

Make sure managers are managing up the senior leaders by providing solid information about their departments. Senior leader rounding is successful because of the middle managers who know their staff best.

14. Should senior leaders round on patients?

Question

Our senior leaders have been rounding on employees for about a year, and now the senior leaders are interested in rounding with our patients. Do you have some advice on the best approach, and are there some benchmark hospitals that have done this with success?

Answer

Yes, many hospitals have been successful with senior leaders rounding on patients. Here are my tips for success:

1. Senior leaders should ask staff to identify candidates for rounding. This takes away the perception that leaders are "checking up on" the department.

2. Senior leaders should look at survey results, and, in coordination with the unit leader, choose one question to ask. For example, if managing pain is the question of focus, say to the staff, "Thank you for asking me to round on Mr. Smith. How are we helping him manage his pain and communicating our efforts to him?" This helps staff describe how they are providing information, handling pain, etc.

3. Have senior leaders always ask some of the same questions. Even though this may seem repetitive, to patients the questions are new. First, senior leaders should outline why they are talking to the patient. If they do not, he or she may feel something is wrong. Comment on staff's commitment to providing very good care when talking to the patient. Then ask a few questions aligned to what staff are working on, such as information, pain, responsiveness, lab, radiology, food,

housekeeping, and other staff who have impacted the patient.
The key is to collect wins, as well as any ideas for improvement.

4. It is crucial that the senior leader take compliments back to staff. I suggest an e-mail to the Leadership Team outlining the experience. Do this each time. This will show what senior leaders are doing, harvest wins, and share ideas for improvement.

Those four steps will help you achieve your goal. It is fine if department leaders or other staff members accompany the senior leaders until they are at ease with the process.

A last caution: don't make a big deal about leaders rounding on patients. In fact, don't place stories or photos of leaders rounding in the newsletter. This makes it look like it's "all for show," when the primary goal of leader rounding is to support our staff.

15.

What do we do if the Leadership Team and the CEO hear conflicting messages during rounds?

Question

My direct reports include leaders for environmental services and food and nutrition. When these two department directors round and review their department scorecards, the departments they rounded on are always positive in their comments. However, when the CEO rounds, everyone opens up with examples of low performance. How can we fix this discrepancy?

Answer

We have found the benefit of the interdepartmental survey is that managers will, over time, relay their concerns openly, thereby reducing the closed-door communications and side conversations. I recommend that the CEO review a copy of the department survey before rounding so that he or she can reference it in response to conflicting information. For example, when the CEO hears a complaint he or she might say, "From reviewing the last survey, I think the department did fairly well. Can I ask what type of feedback you are providing on that tool? The tool is very important for getting leaders to really open up dialogue and make sure we are helping deliver great internal service. I know (name) in that department would want to know this. I also know for those who provide internal service, hearing what is working well is important too."

The CEO must ensure that he or she is not unintentionally creating an I-am-the-only-one-who-can-get-things-done atmosphere because leaders will turn to the CEO with complaints instead of working directly with other department leaders. Instead, I recommend CEOs coach leaders to speak directly with others. The CEO must reinforce the key role of the department leader and urge staff to talk directly to that leader.

Leaders can also reinforce the role of the survey tool as an opportunity to create dialogue on both wins and opportunities for improvement at department meetings and Leadership Development Institutes.

16.

Is rounding on patients simply "checking up on your staff"?

Question

My staff has become hostile that we would dare make patient rounds to find out what kind of care people are receiving. They think we are checking up on them and encouraging patients to complain and get them in trouble. Obviously, this is not our goal. How can we explain our purpose to the staff?

Answer

You may look to see why staff would react like this. It could be an indication of other issues. Do you have some problem employees on your staff? If not, here is my response.

First and foremost, we suggest that leaders round on their staff prior to rounding on patients. Rounding is the number one Must Have^{SM} to drive results, but unit leaders rounding on staff is the most important type of rounding. For the basic questions we suggest leaders ask staff, see Question 9.

When you are ready to round on patients, I suggest that you tell your staff what you'll be doing. Ask them what you should know, what you can do while you are with the patient, and what they have been doing to focus on any key behaviors your department is working on.

Explain to the staff that the goal of visiting patients is to introduce yourself, tell them your expectations, manage up staff members, and harvest reward and recognition opportunities and ideas for process improvement.

An example of managing up is to say, "Your nurse is Linda. Linda has worked on the unit for six years. She is excellent." Do this and your staff will cooperate. In fact, when you are on the unit, they will make sure that you visit patients who have good things to say. If your employees still express worries after you explain this strategy, they may have other issues. Your high performers will adjust and appreciate your efforts.

A last suggestion: Rounding with staff on patients is a great way to build a coaching relationship. When done as described above, challenges with staff will disappear...except with sub-par performers.

17.
Do patients appreciate rounding?

Question

We continue to experience ongoing evidence, through patient satisfaction comments or real-time nonverbal communications, that our patients do not appreciate the manager rounding. Our managers discuss our goals to provide good care, discuss and/or show the survey, or inquire about the patient's stay. How do we improve this process? Or how do we change the focus from the survey to the patient's experience, and still compete with best practice organizations that show the survey and talk about "very goods" and "striving for five"?

Answer

I am going to give you a little pushback on this. My belief is you may be overreacting to a minority of leaders. We have many, many leaders who practice rounding and get great comments. In fact, I round with leaders who are rounding every week. When the rounding is done well, I do not observe a problem.

My perception is that you may have some leaders who are not comfortable with rounding because they are using inappropriate key words. Here is a template to follow:

- Good morning, I'm (name), the nurse manager for this unit. I'm just stopping by to make sure my staff and I are doing everything we can to provide very good care.
- Responding to your requests is important. Have you used your call light? How well are we responding?

- How well are we answering your questions? What about your family and friends? Are we meeting their needs as well?
- Has there been anything about your stay so far that you have been really pleased with? Is there a person I can compliment?
- Please let us know if there is anything we can do for you during your stay. Do not hesitate to ask anyone, including any of my staff or me.

We do not suggest that you "strive for five." We find if the manager communicates interest in providing very good care, manages up staff, corrects any issues, and highlights key questions, the rest takes care of itself.

18. How do you maximize support department rounding for small areas?

Question

I was just reading your article on effective leader rounding, specifically noting your comment that it is imperative that leaders who provide service to other departments round in those areas. I am the marketing/PR coordinator at our facility and a leader. My question to you is: How does my one-person department fit into this picture? What should I be doing to help all of our departments score in the 99th percentile?

Answer

Having served in the same role at one time, here are my thoughts:

1. Round in areas about which you have heard compliments in your community and share these remarks with staff.
2. Find out specifically what patients like about areas with high patient satisfaction. Use the positives in your messages to the community. For example, you might say, "At ABC Hospital, you will be taken to where you want to go and staff will ask you if there is anything they can do for you."
3. Round in the growth areas to see what is being done to create better access for patients. Be part of these efforts.

19.

How can house supervisors round effectively?

Question

I am one of the hospital operations coordinators (nursing supervisor) at a hospital in Baltimore. I attended the Studer Group Institute in November. We would like to start Rounding for Outcomes but are struggling to work this into our role. Any suggestions? What should we be looking for? How and what should we be sending on to the CNO/CEO in the form of reports?

Answer

We always strive to incorporate actions into what is already being done. Let's start with small steps. I believe each week the leader to whom the hospital operations coordinators (HOCs) report should provide them with the following:

1. Areas to compliment. This provides an opportunity for the HOC to say to, for example, the emergency department (ED), "Congratulations, the latest feedback from our patients is that they are feeling much better informed. In fact, you are in the top 20 percent of EDs around the country."

2. A list of tools, supplies, and equipment that have been received based on needs and staff input. "I hear the new scales came. How are they? I am glad administration is so responsive."

3. A question on which to focus: "Administration wants to know what hours you feel are best for food service at night" or "What do you think of the new linen supply system?" The above items can be covered on rounds. I am sure that as you make your way through the hospital you take many notes on issues, etc. I suggest you use a rounding log to organize your notes into

categories such as what's working well, systems that need attention, tool and supply issues, and staff and physicians who deserve recognition.

With the information the HOC gives back, senior leaders can compliment areas that are doing well, fix issues, acquire tools and supplies, and note and recognize individuals. You are the conduit to those many great individuals who work nights and weekends and often miss out on recognition.

20.

What is the best way to approach rounding in ICUs?

Question

I manage a critical care unit with 35 beds. Census is usually 27 to 32. Most of these patients are not alert enough to understand anything I say to them. Trying to round on patients when family members are present is so "hit and miss." What is the best way to approach rounding in ICUs?

Answer

Rounding in the critical care arena has some challenges. The key is to take the concept and adapt it to this setting. First, the leader should round on employees in the unit. Then he or she will be more effective with rounding on patients/family/visitors since the leader will have an up-to-date assessment of any hot spots or issues to act upon.

If this is a unit that has designated visiting hours, these would be the hours for the nurse manager to round. If visiting hours are open, then the nurse manager should round when she believes she will catch most families. It works well for the leader to round in the waiting area periodically as well. A leader for a unit of this type should implement assistant nurse manager rounds or shift supervisor rounds. In this type of rounding, the leader rounds to make sure the patient is comfortable, the family is kept informed, and physician/family/patient/staff communication is excellent regarding progress and treatment plan. In critical care areas, rounding is also important for staying current with evolving situations regarding a specific patient's status.

Another idea is to place the nurse manager's name into a permanent frame. Keep it next to a white board marked with an extension number and a note encouraging family to connect if they need to or have not met the nurse manager.

Many ICU patients are medicated to help ease the trauma of being critically ill and facilitate stabilization of their illness. This makes rounding—and follow-up calls—a challenge. However, follow-up calls for patients/families can be based on a triaged approach: call patients/families when the patient is alert and oriented while on the unit and can provide feedback; call family members of patients who died (sympathy call); call to follow up with patients who have been transferred to an alternate level of care by visiting the step down or med/surg unit just to "check in" to see how they are doing. (This last one is a WOW action!)

21.

How do we improve rounding in outpatient surgery?

Question

I am a manager for the prep and hold area, OR, and PACU. I have recently encountered some difficulty with the rounding process in my prep and hold area. Even the first question about rounding on patients (see Question 17) seems premature, since the patients have been in the hospital only for a few hours and in my unit for about 15 minutes. How can I structure my questions to get good information from my surgical patients? (About 80 percent of our volume is outpatient.)

Answer

You are correct in assuming an immediate post-op question and answer session would be unproductive. Patients have many more important priorities at that moment! One way to alert the patient and family to your interest in providing the best service is a pre-op visit in which you explain that you want to provide great care (use the wording from your patient satisfaction survey to align expectations with results for patients when they complete the survey) and advise them to let you know if at any point they find the care lacking. You can also find out how well the admission and registration process went. Leave your card so they can follow up if you miss them before discharge.

Most likely one of the best ways to capture their feedback is in the discharge callback. This not only provides the opportunity for clinical follow-up but also gives you a chance to manage up staff, identify wins, and capture system or process concerns.

Finally, you can certainly round on patients' families in the waiting area during surgery. They are often the ones to complete the survey and are probably anxious and would appreciate someone checking up on them. Keeping families informed is usually a key driver of satisfaction.

22. How is rounding in an outpatient or physician office setting different from rounding in a traditional hospital setting?

Question

I have been trying to implement patient rounding in multiple outpatient departments on multiple floors. These departments function like MD clinics. Patients are behind closed doors within 15 minutes of their arrival. Families accompany them most of the time. Do you have suggestions on how I might best spend my time?

Answer

In an outpatient setting, round on patients after they are roomed and inform them about the wait if there is one. Be sure to "manage up" physicians when you round (i.e., "You're fortunate to be seeing Dr. Johnson today. He's one of our best and I know he'll want to give you his complete attention as soon as he's available.") Another method for rounding in an outpatient setting is to round in the reception area and ask patients how they are doing. You can offer comfort items like coffee or water or diversion items such as magazines or books.

Also, the leader can identify a certain number of patients and families to approach per week. Identify if they are new or returning. Let the staff know up front that you will be rounding on a certain number of patients and ask them on the day that you round if there are any special issues or things you should be aware of as you round on those patients.

Rounding on patients is a great way to capture what is working well. However, just as with other departments, the most important rounding for a leader is rounding on his own staff. For questions to ask when rounding on staff, see Question 9.

A last note: Some organizations have implemented a postcard survey that patients fill out before leaving. This can be a good "immediate feedback" tool for the staff and physicians. In the outpatient areas, some organizations have even implemented post-visit calls for all new patients to check expectations and service.

23.

Can thank you notes be insincere?

Question

I have worked at my organization for more than 15 years. I received a few thank you notes from my administrator, but they were for trivial matters such as cleaning a coffee machine and running folders to a meeting. These are small things I do every day. I get the impression that the notes are forced, so my supervisor can meet a monthly quota, and very insincere (especially since the same verbiage is used every time).

Answer

There is a learning curve to writing good thank you notes. Yes, the best ones are very specific to behaviors that leaders appreciate most and want to see continued. A gold standard thank you note is also handwritten and mailed to the employee's home.

Here is one excellent example of a thank you note shared with me by an organization:

Dear Elvira,
I can't tell you how touched I was when the patient's baby threw up in the hall and you immediately ran and brought paper towels, comforted the family, and helped clean the mess even though it wasn't your area or department. You truly lived Caring Heart General's value of compassion.

As you have said, it is not rewarding to receive a non-specific thank you note, such as, "Thank you for doing a great job today," or one that recognizes you for doing your job (i.e., "Thank you for covering for me while I was on vacation.").

However, I also urge you to remember that it's often a challenge to even get thank you notes written at times and suggest you exercise some restraint in being overly critical about the quality of these notes. Make it a goal to see progress, not perfection. And focus on the positive.

I also suggest that leaders emphasize the importance of writing thank you's to anyone in the organization when they see an employee do something above and beyond the call of duty (or exhibit a behavior that reflects an important organizational value). I notice there is a tendency for managers to limit their thank you notes to those in their own department, which will not achieve the interdepartmental culture of teamwork that hardwires excellence.

A last thought: let your boss know what you appreciate about him or her. Role model what you want him or her to do for you.

24.

Is there a downside to thank you notes?

Question

Has there been any "downside" to sending notes of thanks to an employee's home?

Answer

No, there is not a downside. I believe that at times even low performers deserve a thank you note. When a leader has counseled a low performer who is trying to improve, a specific thank you that emphasizes actions and behaviors you want to see repeated will reinforce what the employee has done right and increase the likelihood that it will be repeated.

25.

How do you calculate the number of thank you notes to send?

Question

I am looking for the ratio of thank you notes to direct reports. My leadership steering committee seems to think one note per quarter per employee from the manager is okay. What have you found works best?

Answer

Look at the number of staff. I feel every good employee should get at least one handwritten thank you note from the CEO or a senior administrator once every four years. It should include a mention of the manager who praised the recipient. When I was president, I wrote 10 notes a week, 48 weeks a year. We set up a system based on number of staff by unit. By having the senior leader write the note mentioning the manager who shared the information, he or she manages up the entire Leadership Team and creates alignment.

My rule of thumb is to write one thank you note for every 100 employees. For more information on how to set goals for thank you notes and hardwire them into the organization, visit www.studergroup.com and read "The Power of Thank You Notes."

26.

When the manager and peer interviewers don't agree on a candidate for hire, who makes the final decision?

Question

I am currently in the process of hiring a new assistant nurse manager (ANM). The current ANM and I interviewed each candidate, and there was also a separate peer group interview involving five staff members. The problem is that my top candidate is the last choice of the peer group. How can we handle this situation and not lose credibility with the staff?

Answer

Do you have a rating sheet set up by characteristics you are looking for in a candidate? Use one for all interviews. This allows you to go back to the staff and determine whether the candidate behaved differently in the interviews and compare/contrast. You can walk through the ratings and zero in on the differences. This process might make you change your top pick.

A candidate should not be forwarded on to the peer interview if you can't live with having him or her on the team. In short, I would suggest that you go with the staff choice. I find that staff usually have the best sense of a fit in the department and will take personal ownership for that individual's success when they have recommended him or her to join the organization.

27.

What questions should I ask new employees?

Question

We are implementing a 90-day follow-up meeting with new employees to find out how their time has been at the facility and what we could do differently to be more "employee friendly." Can you suggest any questions we should ask during this meeting?

Answer

Yes. I recommend that you ask:

1. How has your experience compared to what we said we were going to be like?
2. What has worked well? What do you like about your job?
3. You still have a fresh pair of eyes. What are some systems, methods, techniques, and so forth from your previous places of employment that might work here? (You're harvesting intellectual capital.)
4. Can you name individuals who have helped you these first 90 days? How have they helped?
5. Are there any reasons you might think of leaving or looking elsewhere?

Don't accept "fine" as an answer—dig deeper. The leader demonstrates accessibility, responsiveness, and the fact that he or she values the contributions of the new hire. Often, issues can be uncovered and addressed early, which will increase employee satisfaction and retention and enhance not only the leader's relationship with the employee, but the strength of the organization as a whole.

New employee meetings at the 30- and 90-day marks are one method of hardwiring the right way to communicate with employees at critical times in their employment. In fact, they typically reduce that first 90-day turnover rate by about two-thirds.

28.

Can you share questions for exit interviews?

Question

Is there a preferred list of exit interview questions that your organization uses?

Answer

We recommend:

1. When you were initially hired, why did you want to work here?
2. What kind of assignments did you most enjoy during your time with us?
3. Did you receive adequate training while you were here?
4. Can you tell me why you want to leave the company?
5. What could we have done differently to keep you here?
6. What did you like most about working here?
7. What did you like least about working here?
8. What are some of the strengths of our organization?
9. What are some of the weaknesses of our organization?
10. Is there any other information you would like to add before you leave?

29.

What if we don't have time to make discharge calls?

Question

All nurses on our staff are to complete approximately five callbacks per shift. How can this rule be enforced? When we are very busy, the nurses just don't get them done.

Answer

Here are a couple of suggestions:

First, we suggest using a format with questions specific to the key words on the patient satisfaction survey tool. Then have one or two of your high performers do their five calls and time each one. Average the length of time the calls take. (Typically, they average two minutes.) This means that you are asking nurses to spend only 10 extra minutes checking on their patients.

Also, keep in front of the staff the actions you are taking as a leader to provide them with this time. Perhaps you are acquiring basic tools and equipment so staff members don't spend time looking for them. Perhaps you get one unit a copier so they don't have to go to another floor. Another area may receive blood pressure cuffs.

When we do discharge phone calls, we eventually get a clinical win. A parent tells us her child who came in the day before with a closed head injury has been sleeping for the last 10 hours. Or we may discover that an elderly man's walker—or worse, his oxygen—was not delivered. Nurses will get their arms around discharge phone calls when they see that such calls can make a positive difference.

In your daily rounding, ask if nurses did their discharge phone calls. Sit at the desk in the morning, and make one or two calls yourself. Managers enjoy hearing the compliments that usually come with the calls. This is great for reward and recognition! (Remember, too, that physicians and physician extenders can do discharge phone calls.) And last, set a goal of how many patients you want to call and how many you hope to reach. If you document progress toward goals and share with staff, they will be more motivated.

30.

How can we prevent multiple calls to patients?

Question

Is there a way to prevent multiple calls to patients after discharge? Not only do the nursing units do follow-up calls, but so do our trauma coordinator, the hospital programs, and therapy.

Answer

You have the right idea to be concerned about patients and their families getting multiple calls after discharge. This can be an irritant, rather than a help.

First, I would recommend identifying all departments that are making these phone calls. This includes all trauma nurses, case managers, social workers, etc. Pull them together for a meeting and include some nurse managers.

Determine the criteria for making post-discharge calls and place multiple department questions into one phone call. This should also include questions regarding service and survey completion so "one call does it all."

Next, set up a process whereby all calls are assigned to specific people. In the case of a trauma patient, the trauma nurse would make that call. Have the unit secretary pull and set aside a face sheet on every discharged patient. This makes it easier for the nurse manager to review at the end of the day and assign the call to the appropriate person. This also gives the manager the opportunity to remove patients from the list who were discharged to a nursing home.

Therefore, the staff members call only the patients for whom they get a face sheet. I would also suggest setting up a process whereby the nurse managers receive feedback from the individuals making the calls. This ensures open communication, which can lead to process improvement and identify reward and recognition opportunities.

31.

How can we make sure discharge phone calls are JCAHO and HIPAA compliant?

Question

JCAHO now says discharge phone calls should be documented in the medical record. I am concerned that this will reduce the number of calls. Any ideas on how to keep JCAHO happy and not overburden nurses, so they will continue to make the calls? Also, what are the implications for HIPAA?

Answer

One method that works well is to create a form that's kept on nursing units in duplicate. The form features a checklist followed by an area to summarize the call focusing on clinical issues. This form can even be the scripted outline of the call, which helps standardize how calls are made by staff. The unit coordinator collects the forms each day and sends them to the medical records department, where they are filed in patients' charts. This method allows the manager to keep a copy for reward and recognition opportunities, process improvement ideas, and so forth.

Another method is to keep the chart on the floor for 24 hours and document calls directly on the chart before it is sent to medical records. If this is not possible, a stamped nurse's note, one labeled with the patient's name, can be retained on a clipboard. It can then be used for the call and sent to medical records.

For HIPAA, we do not see any concerns as long as you take a few steps. Many organizations ask the patient before discharge if they can call her at home as they want to check up with her. This may be documented on a checkbox or may trigger the creation of one of the documents above. You may also ask if you can leave a message. This is documented right on the call sheet that will be used later to call the patient. If a message is left, it should be a standard generic key phrase. Some organizations do not leave messages, but simply note that they made a call attempt on the documentation sheet. Studies—including the article documented below—have shown that up to 19 percent of patients will have some type of adverse reaction within 72 hours of discharge ("Adverse Events After Discharge from Hospital," Feb. 2003 issue of *Annals of Internal Medicine*). Discharge phone calls are critical in improving the clinical outcomes of patients. Adjusting the process for discharge calls to make sure they are compliant with regulations is not difficult and should not be a barrier to hardwiring them.

32.

Is there a benchmark for emergency department callbacks?

Question

We are currently attempting to call all patients who have visited our emergency department. Our success rate at reaching these individuals is about 18 percent. Is there a benchmark by which we can compare ourselves with other hospitals to determine whether this is about average?

Answer

I think 100 percent attempted calls to eligible patients (patients with phones who live in-state and were treated and released) is a great goal. But you will not reach all of these patients, so also set a goal for patients contacted. I recommend a goal of 60 percent contacted, as most of the emergency departments Studer Group works with that are rated in the 90th percentile or above for patient satisfaction are reaching 60 percent or more of patients. You will probably have to make more than one attempt to call many of these patients, during the day and during evening hours, to achieve this level of success. Though it's difficult for staff, early evening is a great time to catch parents who work outside the home and other working adults. I suggest two or three attempts per patient, one in the day, and one in early evening.

Don't call so early or so late that you inconvenience patients. Remember, patients love it when physicians in the emergency department do callbacks, too.

33.

Can you share key words for discharge phone calls?

Question

Are there any key words available for discharge phone calls? We are working on this "Must Have" and would like some ideas to incorporate into ours.

Answer

Key points are:

1. Empathy. "We are calling to see how you are."
2. Clinical questions regarding medications, follow-up appointments, and so forth.
3. "We like to recognize staff and physicians who have done an excellent job. Do you remember any people you would like recognized?"
4. "We want to provide excellent care. How was your care?"
5. "Our goal is to be the best. Do you have any suggestions on things we could improve upon?"

Another tip is to have the key words be part of a log. Staff members will have a guideline to use and can record information at the same time. Don't forget to harvest the recognition opportunities that the patients will share. It makes doing the calls enjoyable for the staff.

For more information, please refer to the article titled "Discharge Phone Calls" at www.studergroup.com.

34.

How do you create buy in for key words (i.e., scripting)?

Question

We need better buy in at our facility for key words. How do we show team members the value of this practice?

Answer

- I suggest you not call it scripting but "key words at key times." Explain to the staff that the purpose is not to get them to change their behavior, but to better explain to patients why they do what they do. Help employees understand that we want patients to know why we do the things we do: to ensure they feel well cared for.

- Select a question and have your staff come up with what they feel are some key words at key times.

- Realize that each leader is a role model. Leaders must use these words and relay back to staff the time savings and efficiency gained by using these key words. For example, a housekeeper says before leaving a room, "Is your room clean for you? Did I miss anything?" Not only will patient satisfaction rise, but as call lights decrease, nurses will have more time when they are not called back into the room because housekeeping missed something. Housekeeping benefits by avoiding two trips to the patient's room. It's a win-win situation.

- By focusing on one question at a time, the results will reveal the right key words for that question. Celebrate, then ask staff to select the next question to work on. (Read "Seven Steps of Driving Results: One Question at a Time" at www.studergroup.com. Just search on "one question at a time.")

- Finally, I recommend that you consider patient satisfaction survey questions as a way to improve patients' perception of core clinical competencies. For example, a key question on most surveys is about pain management. Take the opportunity to connect to clinical staff by saying, "This is how the patients perceive we are managing their pain."

You may also want to read my article "It's Patient Perception of Care—Not a Number" at www.studergroup.com. Search on: "patient perception of care."

35.

How do we measure staff participation in using key words?

Question

We are in the process of implementing key words at key times to reinforce to patients that we want to give them "very good" service/care. Do you have any suggestions for measuring staff participation in using the key words?

Answer

The ultimate measure of compliance, of course, is the result on your patient satisfaction surveys. Until that time, I suggest that when you round on patients, you say, "As your nurse discussed with you, our goal is to make sure you receive very good care." Start by focusing on those employees who you hear are using these key words. The others will fall in line. You can also manage up staff. For example, when entering a patient's room, read on the white board who her nurse is and say, "I see your nurse is Debbie. Debbie has been working on this unit for five years. She is an excellent nurse. Has she discussed our goal of providing you with very good care?"

The last part is to connect the dots for staff on why clear expectations make patients feel more at ease. Of course, this lays the foundation for identifying what very good care looks and feels like to the patient. For example, employees at a hospital in North Carolina say to the patient at the time of admission, "We want to make sure you are satisfied with your care. What are the most important things we need to do to make sure you are very satisfied?" Soon, the results improve, recognition increases, and the Healthcare Flywheel℠ turns even faster.

36.

Are key words for phone answering necessary?

Question

We have introduced key words for phone answering and have encountered major pushback from OR staff regarding internal phone calls. How do I show value in saying, "Good morning, this is the (Name of Hospital) operating room, Patty speaking" when the caller is a fellow employee?

Answer

Explain that just as customers have first impressions, so do staff. Many important interactions take place by phone. A simple name and department identification sets a courteous tone. I would then ask staff if they would appreciate that courtesy.

The best organizations are also looking at closing statements. For example, at the end of each internal call, one human resource department says, "Is there anything more I can do for you?" This has really helped others see the human resource department as a service provider. It also role models.

On another note, when you are implementing such items, consider how you are sequencing them. Don't implement key words for staff to say until leaders have role modeled key words to staff during rounding on employees. Leaders should ask questions such as: "What is working?" "What systems are not working as you would like?" "Do you have the tools and equipment to do your job?" I find that asking these questions to staff will better align their behavior if they have seen improvements that benefit them.

37. Do you have key words for communication with family members?

Question

Some of our patient care managers suggest that our scores are not improving because we are not communicating with our patients' family members. How do we convince our staff that communicating with families is just as important as communicating to patients?

Answer

Communication with family members is vital. In fact, one CEO I know shares a story with new employees during orientation about his own experience as an outpatient for surgery. He says that while his personal interactions with staff were under 30 minutes (he checked in, was prepped for surgery, and had a few interactions with the recovery nurse after waking), his wife was with him for 16 hours interacting with staff the entire time. In this way, he connects the dots for staff that the hospital's customer is more than just the patient. It is the family as well.

Families may impact patient perception of care by up to 50 percent. In the case of most pediatric patients, surveys are completed by their parents. Many children of geriatric patients complete the surveys for their parents.

For inpatient care, at the time of admission, ask the patient about communication and how he or she wants the family involved. It is particularly important that the patient identifies the key contact person to receive information.

A key family member will communicate with the rest of the family, saving staff time. When rounding, have nurse leaders say to the patient, "We want to make sure your family feels it is getting good communication during your stay here. If they have any questions, here is what they can do." At the time of discharge—particularly if family members are involved, as they often are—say, "We want to make sure that you, the family, are kept informed. Are there any questions I can answer?"

In summary: 1. Clear expectations, 2. Key words, 3. Closure upon discharge.

38.

Can you recommend key words for response to call lights?

Question

What would you suggest as a key phrase to say to patients who may have had to wait to have their call lights answered?

Answer

Here are some suggestions:

- Consider an acknowledgment as you enter, such as: "I see that your call light is on. I apologize for my delay. (No excuses.) How may I help you?"
- Follow up with: "I want to provide you with excellent care. Is there anything else I can do for you?"
- Or try: "I am so sorry that you had to wait. Now that I am here, I have time to take care of whatever personal needs you have. How can I make you more comfortable?"
- After you have addressed the need, close the conversation by telling the patient what you are doing to prevent that delay from happening again. "I have asked Mary, your CNA, to check back in an hour or so to see if you need anything."
- The next time you are in the room, make sure to circle back. "Have you had to use your call light?" If it's the next day, ask, "How are we doing on this today?"

39.

Can you suggest some key words to improve bed turnover?

Question

Our facility is small (38 beds), so bed turnover is very important. There are times when we desperately need a bed and we have a patient who is ready to go home, but wants to stay for dinner . . . or one who is waiting for a ride home . . . or one whose baby is in the NICU. How can we use key words at these key times to ask such a patient to give up his room for someone else?

Answer

The first place to use key words is at admission. Explain to the patient and his or her family that your goal is a safe and effective discharge. Throughout the stay, use the goal of the patient leaving as a sign that he or she is getting better. The emphasis is not on giving up a bed, but on becoming well in order to go home.

You may also want to explain to the patient and family that by discharging from the hospital when it is appropriate, they have provided a bed for someone in more need than they are. Include the fact that you will be calling the patient at home to make sure all is well. This phone call will make a big difference. However, if the patient and family are still uneasy, arrange a nursing home visit by a visiting nurse association during the first 72 hours.

Also, providing a checklist of things to do prior to discharge is key for the patient. You can begin referencing this (and discussing a targeted discharge date) early in the hospital stay.

40.

How do we overcome resistance to common key words that all employees are expected to use?

Question

Our Leadership Team decided to roll out the following key words to the entire organization: "Is there anything else I can do for you? I have the time." There has been significant resistance, with comments ranging from, "It doesn't feel natural," to, "You are asking me to lie to the patients by saying I have the time." What is your recommendation regarding modifying the words versus remaining committed to them?

Answer

This is a very common occurrence. We have found that rolling out the key words is harder than developing them. My most important suggestion would be to ensure that prior to asking staff to do this, unit leaders are Rounding for Outcomes with staff. If you haven't connected to what the staff needs, then you will not be successful at hardwiring this behavior. It is important to build the emotional bank account with staff prior to asking them for something. For suggestions on leaders rounding on staff, see Question 9. Once this foundation is in place, here are some suggestions:

1. I wrote an article about developing key words. You can read the article, "Key Words at Key Times," at www.studergroup.com. Just search on "key words."

2. Make sure the senior leadership is behind the key words that are developed, and share success stories in using them at department meetings. The leaders must role model using the key words themselves. It is essential.

3. Develop talking points for supervisors/frontline managers that help them re-introduce the words and discuss why they're important at their department meetings. I have found that when managers ask staff to put themselves in a patient's shoes, they start to realize the difference they can make. Leaders may also discuss how key words may save them time, as patients will not call them back in.

4. Start with: "Is there anything else I can do?" Then, based on senior leadership guidance, decide when to start adding: "I have the time." Remember, it takes the small victories to win the big battle.

5. Ask employees for help in developing the words that work for their particular areas.

6. Look for people who are doing well and reward them. Ask them to share with your team why the key words make them feel better about themselves and the work they are doing.

7. Finally, for the clinical units, you can document the call light usage before and after implementation of these key words. As a result, staff will see how their use of key words decreases call lights.

41. Should evaluations and raises be tied together?

Question

I've read your articles on evaluations, but I'm curious about whether you personally endorse raises that are tied to those evaluations. Or do you believe that pay and evaluations are two separate entities?

Answer

This is an area that has great pluses and minuses on each side. Here is my current thinking: I believe salary and evaluations should be tied together. We recommend using an objective measurement tool, so that just happens naturally. I do suggest that development discussions and development plans take place throughout the year, and that they are not tied to salary but to individual development. I like development planning outside end-of-year evaluation. This way the discussion can focus on development without the emotional pull that a salary discussion can have.

42.

What should we do if leaders give late evaluations?

Question

For approximately six months we have been posting the names of managers who are late in submitting evaluations. We have experienced fair success with this tactic. When you implemented it, did you find that you experienced peaks and valleys in compliance?

Answer

No, I did not experience lack of compliance. Managers knew that the first time they were late, they would be verbally counseled; the second time, they would receive a written notice; the third time, they would be terminated. I find that what gets tolerated becomes acceptable. When you establish zero tolerance for late evaluations, you won't have any.

One CEO tells me that after initial slow compliance for on-time evaluations, his organization has had just one late evaluation in the past five years. This was achieved by deducting points from managers' annual merit increases, printing and announcing their names publicly, and requiring them to meet late at night with the CEO.

CHAPTER 3

HOW DO I BECOME A GREAT LEADER?

Great leaders create great organizations. This means that investing in ongoing leadership training that teaches leader skills and competencies will move you and your organization to the next level. Leadership also drives culture, which determines why employees want to come to work and why they want to stay. (Remember, people don't leave their jobs. They leave their supervisors.)

43.

What is the difference between a "leader" and a "manager"?

Question

I notice that you often use the term "leader" instead of "manager." Is there really a difference or is it just a question of semantics?

Answer

The dictionary defines a manager as someone who "handles, controls, or directs." I see leadership as this and much more. Leaders also:

- Use horizontal thinking: Most leaders are good vertical thinkers. (They know how to impact their own department or implement steps to get a task accomplished.) The art of maximizing people and gains comes in horizontal thinking and communication. How can the information, story, and steps be transferred across the organization? This is horizontal thinking. An example: I remember a department manager who was transitioning to a new vendor for housekeeping service. Not only did he ensure the new leaders were in place, outline the steps to transition, and set clear expectations (vertical thinking), but he thought, "Who else would benefit from this information?" and shared information about the transition to those leaders who had the most day-to-day interaction with housekeeping (horizontal thinking). It's inclusion rather than exclusion.

- Maximize wins: Many times, we fix or improve a situation or issue but we do not go back and connect the dots. We spend hours—or even years—responding to a concern or an issue. Then, instead of leveraging the win, we move to another issue.

With a win, always ask: "What do we need to communicate about this win? When and to whom do we need it communicated? What method needs to be used to communicate effectively?" I feel hospital leaders do many things for which they never get recognized. And I think this often occurs because they are not good at maximizing the win. If patient satisfaction is rising, for instance, it's key for leaders to communicate this to physicians. Otherwise they won't know about steps the hospital is taking to improve the perception of care for their patients.

- Think like the CEO. Whatever your job title is, look for what's working across the organization and duplicate it. Organize lunches or retreats. Take notes at meetings and carry information back to staff. Unit managers can copy best practices on other units. Don't wait. Duplicate what works. If you were the owner of your area, you would not stop until you had great service, high quality, low cost, the best employees, and market growth. Leaders who get results don't need to worry about job security. In fact, they have great autonomy in their role.

- Take a fresh look. Let each day be your first day. An organizational turnaround expert I heard recently explained that while he couldn't replace all of the leaders in the organization, he was invited in because of the poor performance of leaders who were not addressing key issues.

- Aggressively ask for input from staff at all times. While it's not easy, great leaders know that employees are closer to the action and will make or break any change. By asking for input early, the service/product will be better and implementation will go more smoothly. Hardwire rounding on staff (see Question 9 for the five questions to ask).

- Are comfortable with not being comfortable. Role model change for your employees. Today in health care, leaders are going to have to be uncomfortable to achieve quantum improvement in results. When staff and employees are asked to do a job with fewer employees than in the past, the first several months will be uncomfortable. Eventually, directors and managers will change the systems, confront non-performers, and pull together to get the results. The same is true of upper management changes.

- Create "burning platforms" (a sense of urgency). Even success can breed future failure. It is sometimes necessary for all leaders to take a stand and create a platform for increased commitment and a renewed focus of their energy. I have seen CEOs accomplish this in many ways. When they explain the cost of high turnover in dollars lost to the organization, leaders will use tools that create employee loyalty. When staff is held accountable for raising patient satisfaction but it remains stagnant, they will feel urgency to improve service with recommended tools.

- Maximize leader meetings. If you hold such meetings, (and if you don't, please start) use them to reward and recognize leaders, provide information for others, show support, and glean information. When leaders do not routinely attend these meetings, they lose opportunities. They need to represent their area or division and make sure they send notes out to leaders who did not attend.

- Be a player, not a spectator. You do not become the best without passion, ownership, and urgency.

- Reward and recognize. When you let up on this, the results will let up.

- Treasure diversity. Hire a diverse team. Hire people whose skills complement but don't duplicate others. Hire people who want to be students and learn. Diversity is good, so hire it and celebrate it.

44.

How important are mission and vision in cultural transformation?

Question

How important are mission and vision statements in a cultural transformation? Is it imperative that all employees know and understand the organization's mission? Should everyone be able to articulate the vision?

Answer

I think it is important, but disagree with the way most mission and vision statements are written. Sadly, in too many organizations, staff members have heard or seen these statements for years, but are unsure of how they directly apply to their lives. For this reason, many organizations are moving to a simple vision that expresses the organization's desire to be "a great place for patients to get care, physicians to practice, and employees to work."

When I was a hospital CEO, I was most successful when I described this vision in terms of the Five Pillars (People, Service, Quality, Finance, Growth) and supported the vision with clear goals. I then used the employee-driven standards of behavior to help the organization attain the vision. The continuous steps are there to connect behaviors and actions back to organizational goals and standards. This connection makes all the difference.

In summary, it's more important that employees feel they are living a cultural transformation than articulating the vision statement. When a leader asks employees what has changed and they can say they understand the direction of the organization, have noticed low performers no longer work there, or have the supplies and equipment they need, then the leader knows the organization is living its mission and vision.

How can I create a ripple effect as a new director of a unit?

Question

I recently became the new director of a med/surg/peds unit. I believe I am in fact the third or fourth unit director; needless to say, the staff has been through many changes. I am passionate about nursing, and I was hoping you could comment on how I can start a "ripple effect" of positive attitudes.

Answer

Role model, role model, role model! Ask staff what they want the unit to be like. Have them describe what a good unit looks like to them. Then create a unit action plan to make this unit a reality. Get some quick wins and publicize them in a way that isn't self-promotional but informational. This is key. Reward and recognize the behavior you are looking for in your employees. Likewise, don't hesitate to make quick decisions about those with poor attitudes. When a staff member brings up a problem, always ask for her solution before offering yours. Finally, remember that perseverance is important. A cultural transformation that can be sustained will not happen overnight, but your staff will change their attitudes and behaviors if you stay the course. In fact, one of the best ways to change attitudes is to send the names of staff to senior leaders and ask them to recognize employees. When you position staff in a positive light, they will do the same for you.

46.

What level of leader should attend Leadership Development Institutes?

Question

What "level" of leader do you suggest participate in Leadership Development Institutes (LDIs)? Frontline supervisors? Or managers who are somewhat more removed? This question is largely driven by this next one: how many people are too many for these forums to be most effective?

Answer

I believe in being inclusive rather than exclusive. Studer Group recommends that organizations sponsor their own Leadership Development Institutes (two-day leadership development sessions) every 90 days to develop the skills of anyone in a leadership position. LDIs improve individual leadership performance and organizational consistency to hardwire results faster.

In fact, we have organized LDIs for up to 1,200 leaders at a time for organizations that have 13-14,000 staff members. We find if frontline supervisors miss the LDIs, they will end up requiring additional training to ensure success. On the other hand, we have also worked with groups of 50 in smaller hospitals. I also think that when supervisors attend the training, the cultural transformation happens more quickly because they are not dependent on their leader to get them on board.

However, we find it is the work that is done at the LDI (rather than the number of people who attend) that builds a foundation of success. Some questions to think about are: Is the curriculum tied to building competencies for leaders to get the desired results? Is it relevant? Are there pre-work assignments so that the leaders come in prepared for learning? Is post-LDI work assigned to make sure that leaders are hardwiring new behaviors for integration into operations after training? Are specific actions required of different groups of leaders after training?

We have also seen creative LDI Teams divide up the groups depending on the leadership levels so that we could fit the training to their specific needs. The biggest mistake is to assume leaders already have the skills being taught.

47.

What do you recommend that leaders read who are committed to this journey?

Question

Besides *Hardwiring Excellence*, what current written resources would you recommend as essential for managers?

Answer

I recently updated my recommended reading list. Titles that pass the test of time include Jim Collins's *Good to Great: Why Some Companies Make the Leap . . . and Others Don't*, Marcus Buckingham and Curt Coffman's *First, Break All the Rules: What the World's Greatest Managers Do Differently*, and Larry Bossidy's *Execution: The Discipline of Getting Things Done*.

I also write a monthly article geared toward giving very prescriptive "to do's" and practices to leaders. Feedback from managers in the field has been very good. You may find these articles at www.studergroup.com.

CHAPTER 4

HOW CAN I BETTER ENGAGE MY STAFF?

Employees need to believe that their organization has the right purpose. They want to know that their job is worthwhile. They want to make a difference. The best ways to help staff understand the importance of their actions and behaviors are to always connect back to purpose, communicate at all levels, and recognize behaviors you want to be repeated.

What do employees want in a leader? In addition to approachability, they want a leader who will:
- Improve systems to make the workplace more efficient
- Provide tools and equipment to be effective
- Help develop employee skill sets for success
- Request their input on operations
- Recognize and appreciate their work.

Answers to the following questions are designed to help create "engaged leaders."

48. Are there any "best practices" for improving employee satisfaction?

Question

We have just formed a sub-team of our Service Team to look at continuously impacting and improving employee satisfaction. Do you have any "best practice" ideas we should consider first?

Answer

The number one method for continuously improving employee satisfaction and reducing turnover is to hardwire leader rounding on staff. This is not an issue a team can fix. It must happen at the unit level. For information on unit leader rounding, there are many resources organizations may access. A great start would be to review the "Must Haves" chapter of this book.

After beginning unit leader rounding on staff, the next step is to send thank you notes to the homes of high-performing employees. (See Questions 23, 24, and 25 for more information on thank you notes.) As these foundational management practices are being hardwired, make an organizational effort to implement an employee satisfaction survey. In Chapter 7 of *Hardwiring Excellence*, I present a step-by-step approach to rolling out an employee satisfaction tool and responding to the results. This would be an excellent starting point.

These three actions will provide results. Beyond this, I suggest that a team address organizational issues identified in the employee satisfaction survey. These surveys can be done yearly, and mini-surveys focusing on certain questions can be done more frequently to provide direction to the team.

I would also suggest that a sub-team of the Service Team can be helpful, but the real team that needs to address this is the CEO and the Senior Leadership Team.

49.
How much does increased turnover cost the hospital?

Question

I am looking for some ways to measure the costs of poor customer service and teamwork, particularly in terms of employee turnover, for hospitals.

Answer

Estimates of the total cost of losing a single position to turnover range from 30 percent of the yearly salary of the position for hourly employees (Cornell University) to 150 percent, as estimated by the Saratoga Institute and independently by Hewitt Associates.

We feel that it is important for organizations to know the cost of turnover. As you calculate replacement costs, some of the expenses to consider include:

New Hire Costs
- Drug Screens
- Background Checks
- Health Assessment and File Paperwork
- New Employee Orientation—General
- Relocation Expense
- Recruitment Expense—Bringing the employee in for the interview
- Recruiter Expense (External)
- Advertising

Departmental Orientation Costs
Non-nursing
- New Hire (number of hours X average wage)
- Mentor Hours (number of hours X average wage)
Nursing
- New Hire (number of hours X average wage)
- Mentor Hours (number of hours X average wage)

Overtime Costs—for departments covering vacancy

Contract Labor Costs—for replacement for the period of the vacancy

This will give you an estimate of your total replacement costs.

50. How can I make my staff's jobs better?

Question

Based on your advice, I have changed a lot of things that I do. The biggest change I've made is asking people, "What is the one thing that I can do to make your job easier?" I have even incorporated that question into my annual reviews. I ask my doctors and all of my employees.

Most of the time, all I get back is blank stares. I just do not think that people are prepared to answer this question. I find that I get a lot out of spending more time on the floor—sitting at the nurses' station, working the night shift, etc. I see things and ask, "Why is this like this?" I have to lead folks to say, "Hey, that's messed up!"

How do I get my employees to truly think outside of the box—to get away from the mundane—and tell me just what I can change to help them in their work?

Answer

My experience echoes yours. Many employees have shut themselves down after years of not seeing action. I believe people get worn down and stop using their own intellect to solve problems. Here are some tips:

- Bring up observations and ask employees *why*? How does it impact them? What do they think about it? For example, I know a leader who on rounding one Monday asked an employee who had worked over the weekend how it went. Her answer was, "Okay." The leader then asked some specific questions about staffing, ancillary, etc. When they got to supplies, the employee said they ran out of some and had to call for more, but that was normal. It happened every weekend. The leader then asked what the employee felt could be done. The employee said, "We could check census on Friday and adjust inventory based on our expected shortage." They had always stocked the same amount. The leader asked her to talk to staff and decide what levels made sense. The employee had the "Aha!" look. By drilling down, the leader helped the employee return on an engine that had been shut down.

- Select key issues that are problematic and have staff members give suggestions. It's a good way to start.
- Capture things that are excellent and, with your staff, outline the reasons why. Then ask if the same methods might work in other not-as-good areas. You're teaching transfer of learning and techniques.
- When positive ideas and solutions begin to appear, publicize widely. I once invited two lab techs to come to a department meeting to explain how they felt when asked to solve a problem.
- Build into each person's evaluation at least one implemented idea that made the organization better.

51. What kinds of questions can we ask for good interdepartmental feedback?

Question

What kinds of questions can we ask to get interdepartmental feedback to improve the service we give to each other on a day-to-day basis? We have an "Internal Report Card" that we feel could be more useful, with categories such as service attitude, service orientation, communication, and teamwork.

Answer

I recommend questions that speak to:

- Attitude
- Accuracy
- Responsiveness
- Timeliness

Another suggestion: Hold an expectations meeting between department leaders where both rate each other to define the expectations they feel are not always met. If leaders are not aware of the expectations other departments have of them, how can they meet or exceed them? I also recommend that leaders who do such ratings explain how often they use the department.

52.

How can we get people on board?

Question

How do you make this journey contagious and genuine? We have many great minds here who can be quite cynical and who may have been disappointed in the past.

Answer

Making change contagious takes time. Momentum seems to naturally pick up when an organization captures the critical mass. There *will* be skeptics. I find the best way to start is to focus on those who are passionate about making the organization better. Recognize those individuals and units. This creates a gap between those who are on board and those who are opposed or unsure. As those on board move forward, the unsure will move with this group as they see results. The attitudes of the individuals *not* on board will become more obvious. Some of them will then get on board. Others will have a one-on-one meeting with their leader, and choose to get on board or leave as a result.

I find the way to keep the enthusiasm growing is to capture the many wins along the way and communicate wins across the organization. I am frequently asked, "When do people get on board?" In reply, I often suggest leaders learn, "What's the what?" for employees. In other words, the key is to find the one thing that makes all the difference to an individual. For one person, the "what" may be a thank you note mailed to her home. To another person, it may be the fact that his supervisor asked for and acted on his input. For someone else, it may be that her evaluation was completed on time. My last suggestion is to realize culture change is a journey and to connect everything back to purpose, worthwhile work, and making a difference.

53.

How can we keep employee forums valuable and energizing for staff?

Question

Our COO has been conducting employee forums for about one year. At the forums she reviews organizational information and results based upon the Five Pillars. We report the work that work teams are accomplishing and the results of the organizational measures for the Five Pillars.

The time is balanced between reporting and other creative ways of providing information (such as skits, videos that tell "our story," etc.). Since we are interested in taking our organization to the next level, how can we keep our forums valuable and energizing for the staff? What have you seen other organizations do in employee forums to demonstrate an increased focus on ownership, People, Service, Quality, Finance, and Growth?

Answer

Employee forums—quarterly meetings led by senior leaders for all employees—are an excellent way to increase communication at all levels. Here are some ideas I have collected from our national learning lab of hospitals to create maximum impact:

- Collect questions before sessions, both through leaders and in the cafeteria. This way staff will attend to hear their questions answered. If there is not enough time to answer all questions (or some questions are of narrow interest), distribute a printed Q & A on all questions to staff as they join the meeting.
- Ensure that when quality topics are offered, appropriate staff can receive continued education units (CEUs).

- Conduct a mini employee survey at each employee forum, so attendees know they are having impact.
- If the COO is not an engaging, quality speaker, be sure he or she receives presentation training. We find this is important.
- Door prizes are a must.
- Conduct a session for leaders first and get their feedback on what works well and what could be improved. This creates additional ownership.
- Always report on what happened between sessions so that staff understand the impact of their opinions and see the value of completing the survey.
- Make it mandatory that leaders schedule staff to attend.
- Depending on the size of the group, break a large group up into smaller working groups and give them a few minutes to tackle a challenge at the hospital. This helps attendees do real work and give input.
- And last, is the CEO onsite? If so, be sure to have him or her as a presenter.

How can we encourage employees to submit "bright ideas" that are financially sound?

Question

We have a bright ideas program and have received many great ideas from employees. But how do you encourage employees to submit ideas that are financially sound without discouraging them from the program or making them think that the program is only a way to save money? How can we encourage employees to think of ways to better the hospital and not simply enter complaints?

Answer

Instituting a bright ideas program (where employees are asked to share their suggestions for improvements) is an excellent way to create a culture of ownership, harvest the intellectual capital of employees, and generate huge cost savings. It's also important to be able to say no to an idea without saying no to an employee.

Here are a few suggestions:

1. Choose a Pillar to focus on for bright ideas (People, Service, Quality, Finance, or Growth). So if your organization wants to focus on cost-saving ideas, request that employees submit ideas that impact finance in a positive way.

2. Be consistent about publicizing the ideas that are implemented. This way, employees understand what great ideas look like and are inspired to submit them on an ongoing basis because they see that they are actually being implemented.

3. Choose one issue per month (i.e., "How can we increase patient satisfaction?" or "How can we reduce emergency department wait time?") and ask for ideas in those areas.

4. Have a monthly drawing for prizes by Pillar with the same number of prizes awarded in each Pillar. Employees will see that ideas in the Pillars with fewer ideas have a greater chance to win, thus encouraging others to submit additional ideas in those areas.

5. I recommend that for leader evaluations, part of the evaluation be tied to how well the leader meets the expectation that there will be one implemented idea per employee.

6. Explain to staff how cost-saving ideas are used. When you say, for example, that by saving $70,000, the hospital can now afford to upgrade air conditioning in the laundry, cost-saving ideas become less abstract and connect back to making a great place for employees to work, physicians to practice, and patients to receive care.

What are the most difficult issues for a new supervisor in an organization?

Question

What should a new supervisor do to be successful?

Answer

Let me address this question from this angle. These are the reasons I see new leaders struggle:

- They talk way too much about themselves and their last place of work.
- They talk about their area in a way that may be perceived as negative, without seeing value of work done before they arrived on the scene.
- They talk more than they listen. The key is for a new leader to listen to staff and ask, "What do you think?"
- They fail to grab quick wins.
- They don't discuss a specific plan for an area after listening to staff. They don't lay out clear expectations.
- They don't spend time with staff on developing personal relationships. They don't re-recruit.
- They don't address low performance.
- They look self-oriented. For example, a new leader gets new furniture for himself when staff needs are not being met.

Solutions:

- Meet with each staff member and ask what he or she likes about his or her work. What are their ideas for improvement?
- Find a quick win. No win is too small.
- Make sure staff needs come first.

- Spend time learning about each person and discovering what his or her "what" is. In other words, what makes that individual productive and happy? Then deliver it.
- Remove a barrier.
- After listening, run a draft plan for the leader's first 90 days by staff members, based on their feedback.
- Give people credit for the good work they have done.
- Never put down a past leader.

56.

What is the best way to develop a Standards Team?

Question

What is the best way to develop a Standards Team (to set organizationwide standards of employee behavior) within a hospital setting?

Answer

The team should be a cross-section of about 10 hospital employees, including physicians. Because standards will touch the lives of all employees by establishing behaviors that will be expected of everyone, it is important to include representatives of the entire hospital. Members must also be ethical and respected. They must be people who are perceived by their peers as workers who value the mission of the hospital. They must also "walk the talk."

The team must define standards of behavior that will achieve the vision and mission of the hospital. They should develop a commitment statement that lists preferred hospital behaviors for all employees to sign. Then, they must create an ongoing awareness of standards and how they relate to optimal patient care. They need to work with HR on incorporating these standards into both the hiring process and evaluations, and to ensure corrective action policy is in place to support compliance with them. Finally, they need to help individual leaders roll out the standards and help them train their employees to link their behavior to hospital excellence.

Once established, the team should meet weekly until standards are fully implemented. Afterward, they should meet as needed.

57.

What do you recommend regarding the use of 360s in peer reviews?

Question

Our area recently decided to incorporate peer review, sometimes called a "360," in our review process. Do you have a list of questions to use in this type of process?

Answer

Ironically, I was just interviewed by a reporter on 360-degree evaluations. My feeling is that people may be rushing too quickly to the 360 as a review tool. I believe it has merit for feedback for development, but should be seen as just one aspect of an individual's development process. Most organizations are already doing a 270-degree review:

1. The supervisor reviews the employee, often incorporating other aspects of a 360. This is the first 90 degrees.

2. Most organizations do some employee satisfaction surveys. They reflect the employee's perception of the supervisor—the next 90 degrees, putting us up to 180.

3. Most organizations have some type of feedback from customers—that is, patients, physicians, and interdepartmental staff. This brings us to 270 degrees.

4. 360 offers peer-to-peer feedback—the only piece missing. I feel that this last piece is not worth the tremendous financial investment it takes to produce the data.

Most importantly, I believe an organization should look at its review process and ask if an objective evaluation is in place. That said, a 360 *can* have value. But that value is more developmental, and shouldn't be part of the evaluation.

58.

As a working supervisor, how do I approach my staff when handling complaints?

Question

I am the "working supervisor" of a small department. My problem is that I don't know how to approach a staff member when I have a complaint against him or her. In order to counsel staff members, I feel like I need to be in "boss" role, but because I must also work shoulder to shoulder with them, I don't want to cause any strain between us. How do I tactfully broach a sensitive issue with them?

Answer

Employees appreciate a supervisor who understands the job and will work shoulder to shoulder with them. Your role brings about some advantages as well as the disadvantage you have expressed. Although you are working with staff, you are still a supervisor. If people are doing a good job, there will not be a strain. So, the key is to develop the skill set to coach and confront staff performance. Here are some tips that have worked for me:

- Make sure staff know what the desired outcome is.
- Actively and publicly recognize staff who are doing good work.
- Use the *support, coach, support* approach when intervening early with staff. For example, say to Judy (employee), "I want to compliment you on the way you organized your work today. Although, I did notice that you tended to get off task, which delayed our ability to call the physician back. I know you are committed to doing this, so let me give you some suggestions that might help. Once again, the way you organized your work today was excellent." The more you practice this approach, the better you get.

Additionally, when I was in your situation, I found that I needed to look in the mirror and ask myself, "Am I acting like a supervisor when it is advantageous to me and abandoning that role when it feels uncomfortable?" A working supervisor is a supervisor at all times in the eyes of employees.

How do we handle anonymous complaints?

Question

How do you handle anonymous complaints made against specific Management Team members? In our case, these take the form of anonymous letters to the administration. The charges are incorrect and cannot be validated.

Answer

Unless the complaints involve ethical issues that need to be addressed, I would ignore them. In my two-day sessions, I teach leaders how to address situations like this, and also discuss *why* people come in with statements such as, "I can't tell you who said this but …" Incidents like this are another reason why I feel employee surveys are so important. They give all staff members the opportunity to weigh in. I don't have respect for people who can't sign their name, and paying attention to such anonymous things (like the aforementioned letters) only reinforces secrets and child-like behavior.

How can I recognize and reward non-patient care staff?

Question

Our Customer Excellence Team is struggling with ways to recognize and reward non-patient care areas that are not part of the patient satisfaction survey process—finance, information systems, material management, etc. We are wondering about specific criteria, tracking systems, reward ideas, and lessons learned. Can you give us any guidance or "best practices"?

Answer

First, you might be surprised to know that many organizations receive positive comments about individuals in admitting, housekeeping, maintenance, insurance verification, the business office, and other non-patient care areas who interact by phone with patients on their patient satisfaction surveys. Organizations then harvest these for reward and recognition.

Here are some suggestions on other ways to recognize them:
- Many organizations have created a monthly process in which patient care areas evaluate non-patient care areas. This leads to process improvement and helps with reward and recognition.
- Ask the nurse leaders when rounding to ask staff which systems are working well, which other departments they found helpful, and why. The leader harvests these positives and connects with the departments mentioned to recognize their results. This creates more desired behavior and creates goodwill between departments.

- A key reason we suggest hardwiring employee thank you notes is to include areas that do not get mentioned on patient survey tools and in letters from patients. For example, the director of medical records sends the CEO a note about the super work a transcriptionist is doing. The CEO then sends a note to the transcriptionist's home thanking her for what she does and pointing out how it makes a difference.

- Whenever a patient care area gets named on a survey, mentioned in a letter, or hits a performance goal and is rewarded, double the reward. Then, have the patient care area staff give the "extra" half to those in a non-patient care area that they feel contributed to the results.

- Similarly, some organizations have programs where employees can exchange commendation letters (initiated by any employee!) for gifts, such as movie theater gift certificates. This is an excellent way to highlight high-performing individuals who don't work directly with patients.

- At department meetings and quarterly employee forums, have senior leaders "connect the dots" for those who they don't work directly with about the difference they make.

- Each month or quarter, have direct patient care areas select a "support department of the month." For example, skilled nursing picks linen because that department is critical to preventing pressure ulcers. Then, linen gets a prize. I know one nursing unit that bought food for the linen department and "connected the dots" on how critical they were to patient care.

- Finally, recognize an employee of the month, expanding the honor to include a person under each of the Pillars of People, Service, Quality, Finance, and Growth. This way, people in departments that do not directly touch a patient can be recognized.

61.

How do we provide recognition for night shift employees?

Question

I have been on the Recognition and Recovery Team for over a year now. I enjoy being on the team and doing the rounding, but lately we have been getting complaints that we do not recognize people on the night shift.

Answer

Treating all employees equally is very important. Here's how:

- Make sure the night shift has their "own" food. For example, if you give baskets of candy to the unit for raising their scores, have a separate one for each shift, labeled as such so it does not get eaten by others.
- Have the night shift designate a "liaison" to serve on the team. They do not have to attend all the meetings, but they get the minutes and serve as the communication link.
- Rotate the meeting time once per quarter and invite the night shift people to attend as guests.
- Take turns rounding on the night shift and handing out ice cream bars or some other item to each employee. "Connect the dots" on why you are doing it.
- Ask the Executive Team to take turns rounding once a month on the night shift. For example, every third Thursday at 2 a.m., a member of the Executive Team will round on the hospital night shift workers.

- The most instrumental person on the night shift tends to be a house shift supervisor. Make sure that each week this individual has a list of the wins (i.e., tools and equipment that have been purchased or fixed) so when she rounds, she can reinforce the win with the staff. Also, ask her to send in reports after each shift identifying staff and physicians who can be recognized.

62.

How can we motivate staff to use white boards consistently?

Question

Although we have tried, we cannot seem to successfully motivate our staff to use and update white boards we have placed in patient rooms to keep patients updated on their nurse's name/extension and other information that helps them feel informed about their care. Do you have suggestions?

Answer

I am not sure that it is a matter of motivation as much as it is how well the manager of the unit sets expectations. If you are struggling with staff compliance, I would suggest the following:

For 30 days, have the manager/charge nurse take responsibility to make sure the boards are updated each day. Then when the leader rounds on the patients and families, ask them, "Do you find it helpful to have the board updated with the nurse's name?"

You will find that they often say, "Oh yes, very helpful. As a matter of fact, it's the first thing I look for when I come in." You can then share these specific patient comments to help staff understand why you are setting the expectation that white boards stay current.

Next, approach the staff by saying, "For the last 30 days I have made it my personal mission to be sure the white boards are updated. Let me share with you some of the comments our patients and families have made about this. (Give the examples you have collected.) Because this is an important way of sharing information with our patients, I am going to expect that the white boards be updated each shift and that each of you take on this responsibility as you introduce yourself to the patient. The charge nurses and I will be monitoring to be sure we get this important task completed for the safety and comfort of our patients."

63. How can I continue to buy in when my supervisor doesn't?

Question

Personally, I believe in your Nine Principles® to creating a Culture of Excellence, but my VP doesn't believe in this approach. Explain to me why I should once again attempt to be a leader when the person I work for doesn't support my efforts.

Answer

Do the best you can to be a great leader for your area, even if it has limited impact in the organization. I believe you wouldn't be writing to me if you weren't already a good leader and that you hold strong personal values that won't let you work any other way. I have seen one instance when a leader had such great results in her own area, and the CEO was so impressed, that the whole organization got on board. So, short-term, be the best leader you can be. Long-term, if you can, try to find an organization that will embrace your desire. There are many out there. I doubt that your VP will be a long-term player.

How can we help other leaders hold up the mirror?

Question

We are embarking on the quality journey and have certain department directors who think they get it, but in reality they aren't even close. How do we help them recognize that their autocratic style doesn't fit the new reality?

Answer

Your best indicator is to look at staff turnover, staff satisfaction, and exit interviews. Hard data is what works. All three of those will provide a fair picture of whether or not department directors "get it."

I recommend holding staff focus groups to describe the type of leadership they are looking for. In all likelihood, the staff will lay out a very fair and practical description. Leaders will be expected to follow the agreed upon standards of behavior.

Finally, it is valuable to have senior leaders outline what they see as the characteristics of a great leader in the organization.

What do I do if I disagree with my supervisor's opinion of my performance?

Question

I do report development for my supervisor, who recently mentioned to me that I have not been completing this responsibility on time. But I get the requests in bunches and am given only a short time to complete them.

The fact is, supervisory retaliation occurs in my organization. How do I express myself to management without fear of losing my job?

Answer

First, if retribution takes place, you should leave and go to a better place to work. If you can't, then be the best you can be each day.

Here is how I would handle your situation:

Make an appointment to see the boss and say, "Thanks for your feedback on the reports. My goal is to exceed your expectations. I want to propose a system that will ensure the reports are done to your satisfaction."

Then, lay out a Gant Chart (a tool that can help plan, coordinate, and track tasks in a project) that details when a report comes in, the time required to turn it around, and tracking. Tell your boss, "These are my thoughts for improvement, but of course I will appreciate any and all suggestions you have and ask you to review this plan."

This is a win-win situation. It shows you as a solution carrier, and it will work if done in a non-accusatory fashion.

How can I work more efficiently reporting to multiple leaders?

Question

Do you have some advice on working with multiple managers and a large number of employees? I am a department secretary and I handle plenty of issues in my department. I am an assistant to my director and two coordinators. I also make sure that the employees are taken care of. Do you have any advice on how to work with multiple managers with minimal stress?

Answer

I don't have a magic bullet. I do have a suggestion, which is to sit down with each manager and ask, "What are your critical priorities?" Then, show the different managers all the priorities and ask, "What could be standardized?" Then, once they understand the critical success factors, ask them to identify for you what could fall off the plate without critical consequences. Do this and I think you'll see an improvement.

67.

What is your advice for performance appraisals for frontline employees?

Question

We have established a team to redesign our performance appraisals for frontline employees. We want these appraisals to be effective and meaningful to employees and managers alike. Any advice?

Answer

To start, identify expectations on the part of the manager and employee when they do sit down together. Then, review the overall performance of the department first, so the employee can see how he or she has impacted the department's performance. If you want to retain this particular employee, first say, "You are a valuable employee and we want to retain you." Then, review all positive contributions the employee has made. If developmental suggestions are necessary, the manager should cover those and brainstorm with the employee on improvements. The manager needs to end with an outline for herself on what she can do to help the employee improve.

Remember, the goal is to give continuous feedback during rounding and also within the high, middle, and low performer conversation framework. Remember, this once-a-year process is just one part of an ongoing dialogue with staff throughout the year.

68. **How can we ensure our efforts speak to all cultures?**

Question

I have a situation in which the entire customer service initiative is very difficult for employees from certain cultures. Do you have any information on customer service and cultural diversity in the workplace?

Answer

Many organizations have a "Cultural Diversity" Team, which is a good way to help people learn, respect, and integrate their differences. Some organizations have used these differences to "excuse" how certain staff members perform. Obviously, there should be no excuses in regard to poor customer service. To provide coaching and training for staff, some organizations have created "lab settings" where employees can practice skills that they are expected to perform in the patient environment. Role-playing is an effective tool for learning.

One day, I was among a team of leaders at an organization in San Francisco, one of the most culturally diverse areas in the U.S. Leaders were addressing their concerns about the impact of a diverse workforce and a diverse patient population. The COO shared his viewpoint: "We are creating our own culture within our organization that will provide the best care for our patients, the best place for our staff to work, and the best place for our physicians to practice. We need everyone on board." I agree.

69.

How can we fill nursing leadership positions on an interim basis?

Question

Our patient satisfaction scores are at an all-time high: the 85th percentile. Our challenge, however, is turnover at the nursing director and manager level. Have you seen any good interim solutions (i.e., outside help) to temporarily fill positions in organizations focused on continued culture change?

Answer

If the vacancy is temporary, see if someone in the organization can take over, even if he or she is not experienced in that area. I have even seen a non-nurse be a good interim leader on nursing units. There are many leaders in support departments such as PT that have made excellent interim leaders.

Another suggestion is to gather the nursing staff together, tell them you need an interim leader, and ask for their suggestions. Staff members often know their peers better than anyone else, and if they pick their own interim leader, that person is more likely to be successful.

An exercise you may want to consider doing is what I call "What's In/What's Out." Have the staff break up into groups and determine what behavior is acceptable for their department and what is unacceptable. For example, offering to help a peer who looks like he's in need may be "in." Managing down another staff member may be "out." This is a good exercise to help increase the maturity of the team, especially during an interim leader basis. For more on this exercise, go to www.studergroup.com and search for the article titled "Do We Filter out the Positives?"

70.

What role do volunteers play?

Question

I am the director of volunteer and pastoral services at our hospital. I automatically applied everything you said to both my departments. I feel that the Nine Principles® are just as applicable to volunteers as they are to employees and physicians. How does the role of volunteers differ from that of physicians and employees in the overall journey to developing an excellence-based culture?

Answer

I really don't see a difference between volunteers and employees, except we need to appreciate that volunteers act like employees but receive no payment for the service they provide. You can use the materials, tools, and techniques taught at Studer Group's Institutes for both. I would suggest being "extra grateful" for the time and efforts of your volunteers and constantly rewarding and recognizing them for their great work. I suggest that all leaders round on volunteers to their departments and express their appreciation for their valuable contribution.

CHAPTER 5

WHY IS MEASURING RESULTS SO IMPORTANT?

Measurement supports organizational alignment of desired behaviors, holds individuals accountable for results, and ensures an objective way to assess progress towards goals. We do not measure just to measure. We measure to align specific leadership and employee behaviors that cascade through the organization to drive results. The better you can align behaviors, the more quickly you will achieve results.

71.

How should the strategic plan align with the Five Pillars?

Question

How closely should a hospital's strategic plan align with the Pillars? Or can the Pillars themselves be used as the basis of the strategic plan?

Answer

The Pillars (People, Service, Quality, Finance, and Growth) should be the foundation of the strategic plan because they ensure that goals are balanced and help the organization set priorities to achieve those goals. From the strategic plan, the organization can set annual goals that then cascade down to leadership. That is what I call organizational alignment. (To learn more about organizational alignment and the Five Pillars, go to www.studergroup.com; search on "organizational alignment" to read my article titled "Sustaining the Gains: Creating Organizational Alignment through Accountability," that appeared in the May/June 2002 issue of Press Ganey's *Satisfaction Monitor*.)

On another note, I think many organizations get confused between strategies and tactics. For example, if the goal is to be the best provider of choice in the market (strategy), the next step would be to set targets by Pillar that will be needed to hit the strategic goal.

Under each target are the tactics to get there. Here is an example of how to apply the process:

1. On an annual basis—at the very top level of management— establish and communicate one to two numeric goals for each of The Pillars. Some sample goals:

- Growth—Gain market share in the eastern quadrant of the service area and/or increase outpatient volume 30%.
- People—Reduce RN turnover four points and/or increase employee satisfaction for first year employees by five points.

The idea is that top management needs to study the statistics from management reports and determine what is important for the organization to focus on in the coming year to set goals that are clear, precise, and measurable.

2. Next, tactics are developed to meet these numerical strategic goals. Some sample tactics:
- Growth—To grow market share, establish a primary care clinic, recruit a primary care practice in the eastern quadrant, or develop a new outpatient facility that focuses on customer service and technology.
- People—Make changes in orientation, begin management rounding, do pulse checks at 30/60/90 days, or implement peer interviewing.

Here, the idea is that there are probably four to seven tactics that the organization can implement to help achieve the overall strategic goals. (Many more than that can't receive proper implementation guidance by top management.)

3. Finally, ask individual departments to develop plans on how they can best contribute to implementing the tactic. Some examples:
- The cardiology department may work with cardiologists to identify internists in the east who can be recruited, or help host heart screening events at the mall in the east to attract patients.
- The radiology department may identify new equipment needs that would increase referrals from internists—an open MRI, for example.

- The nursing units may develop a process to hardwire the pulse checks, and the HR department may designate "Interview Saturdays" to allow for peer interviews in slow periods.
- All departments can be involved with this approach and all employees can understand the organization's goals. This ensures the plan is monitored, comprehensive, and detailed.

Of course, the plan needs to be monitored and modified, the results celebrated, and lack of follow-through addressed, but with careful implementation, organizations will see success across all Five Pillars. Organizations that make the commitment to link The Pillars to strategic planning really start the flywheel turning.

72.

What are good yearly goals for facilities?

Question

In completing goals for 2004, using the Five Pillars (People, Service, Quality, Finance, and Growth) as guidelines, what are some examples of good goals for non-patient care areas such as facility management? I have tied service back to satisfaction surveys, but have hit a roadblock with some of the others.

Answer

Here are a few sample metrics that are often used in plant operations and maintenance:

Finance - Budget/Operating Expenses
Finance - Worked Hours/Unit of Service
Finance - Utility Expenses
Finance - Overtime Expenses
Growth - Square Feet Serviced
People - Employee Turnover Percentage
People - Employee Satisfaction Survey Results
Quality - Preventative Maintenance Percent of Service Requests
Quality - Service Call Rework
Service - Interdepartmental Satisfaction Score

There may be other metrics out there that you might wish to set goals around; these are simply the more common ones. You can set Pillar goals for every department.

73.

How can we better create accountability in our organization?

Question

I am a manager in an organization in which a safety issue is not being addressed appropriately. Here is what happened: an employee filled out an incident report and sent it to his supervisor, environmental manager, quality manager, and CEO by e-mail. However, twelve days have passed and nothing has been done.

I feel that as a manager of the hospital, I am accountable to this employee, who is frustrated because he followed the chain of command, yet no action was taken. Some managers here talk the talk, but don't walk the walk. In *Hardwiring Excellence,* you emphasize the importance of follow-through by managers in creating accountability. How can I make such follow-through happen?

Answer

The problem may be that there are so many hand-offs that appropriate follow-up rarely gets done. I do recommend that when several individuals are copied on a letter of complaint, a single individual is clearly assigned to be responsible for coordinating an investigation and response.

In cases where no action is being taken, I suggest you approach the person who you feel is best positioned to handle this concern and use the "support, confront, support" technique.

Start with some positive statements. This will create a less defensive reaction. Then, say something like, "There is probably a good reason why you have not heard about this. I know that you are aware of the organization's commitment to safety and would like to communicate with the employee in response to his concerns."

My guess is that the assertive action, combined with this tactful approach, will get you the information you need. Then, finish with supportive comments. It's important that you don't set up a "we/they" mentality between employees and other leaders.

Incidentally, you may need to rethink the ways that you communicate. E-mail can be a useful tool, but sometimes it creates too many hand-offs with ill-defined accountability. Finally, realize that taking action in the way I just described will role model adult solution finding for the rest of your team.

74.

How quickly should accountability be hardwired into the leader evaluation process?

Question

How quickly—within how many months—should accountability be "hardwired" into an organization's evaluation processes? How much input should middle managers have into this process?

Answer

I recommend you make it a goal to have accountability hardwired—by using an objective leadership evaluation tool—no later than the first time annual reviews are due after putting the Five Pillar process in place. In fact, the sooner the better! It is important to introduce the new tool immediately, as it does take time to implement. Many organizations choose to begin by introducing Studer Group's leadership evaluation tool and also integrating any other evaluation tool they are using as best they can until the new tool is fully operational. I feel middle managers' involvement in weighting goals and assigning the one to five performance scale is crucial since they are closest to what they do. However, some of their recommendations may be non-negotiable. The senior leadership team may need to make adjustments to assure the organization hits the desired goals.

Should leaders be held accountable for unit-specific results?

Question

We use a patient satisfaction survey tool and patient satisfaction is now tied to annual management compensation. We would like to set a separate goal (based on our organization's percentile ranking) for each area/department that takes into consideration its unique ability to drive the overall score upward...rather than setting each department's goal at the overall outpatient or inpatient goal. What are your feelings on this?

Answer

I think there are two approaches that both have merit. On one hand, it is nice when each unit has its own goal based on past performance and desired outcome. The good news is that by using the percentile, it will actually be fair for each department. For example, a nursing unit may have a higher mean score than food services, yet food services may have a higher percentile ranking.

Another example might be that a nursing medical unit might have a lower mean than another non-medical nursing unit. Yet, compared to all medical units, that unit might have a high percentile. In fact, a highly perceived medical unit is a great advantage because of its large impact on overall percentile ratings. That's how percentile rankings create fair evaluation of results.

On the other hand, I also know organizations that have been very successful by basing rewards on overall hospital scores to encourage a "one for all and all for one" mentality.

76.

How can we foster open communication with our customers about patient satisfaction results when our results are less than desired?

Question

We have recently developed communication boards throughout the hospital using the Five Pillars—People, Service, Quality, Finance, and Growth—which is wonderful. However, we are struggling with posting percentile rankings that are less than desirable (i.e., 30s and 40s). Our concern is that the public and many of the employees reading this information on the board do not understand the meaning of the rank.

Answer

Posting poor results in public areas of the hospital is never easy for any organization. However, I find that informative communication boards that give frequently updated data on key benchmarks under each Pillar do inspire staff and create accountability. (The key is to make the communication boards less about the graphics, and more about the content.)

It's true that word of mouth is critical in attracting patients to the hospital, but many organizations recognize that the community already knows they have much work to do. So they do post scores publicly to signal their commitment to getting better.

If you are concerned that employees or patients may not understand the difference between mean scores (how patients rated you on the survey) and percentile rankings (which compares your organization to others), consider using the raw score with the percentile ranking next to it. I know it's not easy, but it does create urgency for improvement.

The other avenue is to have the more public communication boards focus on staff, while the Five Pillar boards in units share ranking information.

77.

How can we communicate dashboard data in a timely fashion?

Question

We would like to provide a one-page dashboard with a weekly summary of pertinent information for hospital executives, directors, and managers—possibly using a pop-up screen on their PCs. What metrics would you suggest we include? What other ideas do you have for communicating this type of information on a timely basis?

Answer

I like the idea of a pop-up screen that would provide the following indicators based on how frequently the information is available. Keep in mind that many other things could be tracked as well. Below, I have focused only on the most important.

People:
- Turnover—RN, non-RN, and total (updated monthly)
- Ninety-day turnover (updated monthly)
- Staffing productivity (updated biweekly)

Service:
- Satisfaction scores by area (updated weekly and monthly)

Finance:
- Budget variance (updated monthly)
- AR days (updated daily)
- Net operating income (updated monthly)

Quality:
- One or several of your top quality metrics (mostly updated monthly)

Growth:
- Admissions by unit (updated daily)
- OR visits (updated daily)
- ED visits (updated daily)

CHAPTER 6

HOW CAN I RAISE PATIENT SATISFACTION?

Patient satisfaction flows naturally from employee satisfaction. The two are interwoven. When you connect organizational values to actions, you get results. This chapter shares ways to increase employee ownership of patient satisfaction results and better respond to patient needs.

78.

What's the best way to make gains in patient satisfaction?

Question

Our patient satisfaction is low—with scores in the mid-twenties or below. I want to address this, but I'm just not sure where to start. What do you recommend?

Answer

I recommend you begin by focusing on one question at a time. In essence, ask nurse leaders to choose and focus on just one question from the organization's patient satisfaction survey that has the biggest impact on patients' overall perception of care and willingness to return or recommend, such as, "Those with me were kept informed."

Next steps explain how leaders can connect for staff the use of key words and key actions to improvement in this area. Then coach those employees who need to improve and recognize those who excel.

I recommend you read my article "Seven Steps of Driving Patient Satisfaction: One Question at a Time" at www.studergroup.com. It explains in detail this sequenced, step-by-step approach to improving patients' perception of care.

79.

Is 100 percent satisfaction possible?

Question

Can you achieve 100 percent patient satisfaction? Can you measure it?

Answer

My experience tells me that there will not be a time when 100 percent of your patients will rate their care tops in every category every time.

For organizations using a five-point scale for patients to rate their satisfaction (with five being the highest), those that rank at the top have about 74 percent of patients rate them a five. Sixteen percent rate their care a four. Seven percent rate their care a three. Two percent rate their care a two, and one percent rate their care a one. For organizations using a ten-point scale for patients (with ten being the highest), I have found 90 percent rate their care a nine or ten. Eight percent rate their care a six to eight and two percent rate care a one to five.

The key is to move the patients who rate their care "good" to the "very good" category. This could also be moving patients from "satisfied" to "very satisfied," depending on the measurement tool used. The focus is to move the second-best rating to the best.

80. Realistically, how high should we set our patient satisfaction score goals?

Question

As an institution, our strategic planning objective for this year is to improve our patient satisfaction scores. Our most recent overall ranking is in the 29th percentile. We want to set a goal for next year but are not sure what we should target. Some believe the 50th percentile would be doable; others want nothing less than the 75th.

Answer

Because it's a bell curve system, it's not impossible to move up to the 75th percentile in setting your score. To do that, I believe an organization has to be committed to leadership development and changing the leadership evaluation system. Before making the decision, look at your medical surgery unit scores. The med surg unit (because of the higher number of discharges, and, thus, patient surveys) has more influence in your percentiles. Review the med surg unit scores and see if you feel confident that you can move those scores past your goal. I'm not saying what your goal should be; I'm saying that before setting your goal you should do a little more research. I feel that at the 29th percentile, your organization may need to address other issues beyond patient satisfaction.

81.

How can we increase employee ownership of the patient survey tool?

Question

At our hospital we have low staff buy in and ownership of the patient satisfaction surveys. The process doesn't mean anything to the staff. I would like to know things that managers can do to get buy in for the patient satisfaction surveys.

Answer

Here are some quick tips:

- Call the results "The Patients' and Families' Perception of Care." In radiology, we don't call the MRI results the Phillip, or some other vendor name. By referencing the survey tool by vendor, you remove the people who fill it in from the equation. When I am in a hospital, I ask the staff if they know what everyone who fills in a survey has in common. The answer? They have all been touched by someone at the hospital. Connect the patient to the staff, not to the vendor or tool.

- Read the questions to the staff. The questions are not about minor issues but core clinical competencies. The competencies are response to call lights, management of pain, information about care, and home care instructions. It is crucial that the leader connect the survey back to staff.

- Look for the good. When a patient is admitted, assure her that you want to provide very good care. Discuss what the patient and her family feel that care will look like. This allows the staff to know what the patient is looking for and provides time for education of patient and family.

- Focus staff on one question and how they can improve patient perception of that particular area. An article at www.studergroup.com, "One Question at a Time," provides this framework.

- In discharge phone calls, let the patient know you like to recognize staff members who have provided very good care. Collect names and recognize these staff members. Then let the person know he will be getting a survey and should complete it as it helps you capture what went well and identifies areas that need improvement. Encourage him to write any names of staff members he would like to see recognized.

- Use percentile comparisons, not raw or mean score. Staff will more easily see this move.

- Look at results weekly. When you see good weeks, recognize staff and review what is being done to get such positive feedback. This creates a success template. It helps you determine what's working.

Also, I recommend you read my article "It's Patient Perception of Care—Not a Number" on www.studergroup.com for actionable information as it addresses this very issue.

82.

What strategies can we use to increase response rates to surveys?

Question

I would like to encourage my patients to participate in the patient satisfaction survey they receive when discharged. What type of strategies do we use to prevent it from appearing that we are, as a unit, formally soliciting their opinions?

Answer

I have found that discussing the survey with the patient while still at the hospital is beneficial. One health care organization did an interesting thing. They gave a handout to patients that said it was time for a check-up and explained that they needed information to improve. It highlighted that they may get a survey in the mail. It also said if the hospital isn't providing very good service at any time, not to wait until the survey came, but to let them know right away.

This information can be given when patients are admitted to your floor. My recommendation is to not worry about intruding or asking. We have found that patients want to hear that you care about what they think, that you want to improve, and that you appreciate their feedback!

Finally, as part of discharge phone calls, you can let patients know that they will be receiving a survey in the mail and you appreciate their input as it helps the organization provide very good care. When doing the discharge phone calls, let the patients know this does not replace the survey and you would very much appreciate their filling it out and returning it.

83. What is the role of patient relations?

Question

What is the legitimate role of a patient relations department? In my job, patient relations reports to me. I also have human resources, the volunteers, pastoral care, and operations improvement (Six Sigma approach). You have commented that the first thing an administrator often does is hire a patient representative to keep those complaining people away from him or her. If that is the purpose, I would do away with our patient reps and make nursing and administration deal with complaints directly. I believe that a patient relations representative does have a legitimate role but would appreciate your thoughts on what that role might be.

Answer

I agree with you. Unit leaders need to deal with complaints, especially if the patient and family desire that administration deal with complaints. I see the role of patient relations as centered on understanding the measurement tool and educating leaders on what to focus on to improve service. These people should be involved in trending complaints for use in process improvement. They should harvest the tools and techniques that work and use them in developing leaders' skill sets. They should research what to do next.

84.

Does the rating point scale on the patient satisfaction tool matter?

Question

Our hospital has used a four-point satisfaction scale for the last decade. However, we are really working on our key drivers of satisfaction. I feel that the four-point scale will not really show our efforts of improvement as much as a five-point or higher scale. Further, is it better to label the scale (Very Satisfied, Satisfied, Somewhat Dissatisfied, Very Dissatisfied...) or simply ask patients to give a number one to five, where five is "completely satisfied" and one is "not satisfied"?

Answer

The "verbiage" and point scale will be whatever your vendor has selected. The important point is to become very knowledgeable and comfortable with the tool and to have staff using the language of the tool as they go about creating a culture that will focus on customer satisfaction. Most tools have questions that pinpoint the eight to ten things that are most important to patients. I don't believe the importance lies with the numeric scale but rather with meeting the needs that the survey tools list, and measuring ourselves against others in an "apples to apples" approach.

85.

Should we focus on employee or patient satisfaction first?

Question

We are developing our Service Teams, which include several areas like patient, employee, volunteer, and physician satisfaction. Is there a sequence to follow? Should we focus the majority of our energy on employee satisfaction before we move to patient satisfaction, at least in the first year of our committee?

Answer

Make sure you have measurement in place on employee turnover and patient satisfaction. I would focus on employees first, until you see lower turnover. This can take from three to nine months.

By Rounding for Outcomes (especially by unit leaders) and implementing thank you notes effectively, you will build a bank account of trust with employees. When they feel they have the tools and equipment they need to do their jobs (or understand why these cannot be made available), have a solid relationship with their supervisor, and feel rewarded and recognized, they will be ready and willing to take prescriptive steps to increase patient satisfaction.

86.

How can the emergency department (ED) institute a new mentality?

Question

I am an ED nurse in a mostly chaotic emergency department. Our manager and medical director have recently attended one of your seminars and converted to your philosophy. Our ED historically has an overall poor customer satisfaction rating but receives higher marks for quality technical medical care. I understand that these are two different aspects of providing quality health care, but I am having a more difficult time adjusting to the concept of "consumerism in medicine." Any suggestions for those of us who have always believed that the ED is for highly skilled medical care and stabilization?

Answer

While this is a common feeling among many emergency department staff, service and quality are not two different aspects of the ED. Indeed, they go hand-in-hand in delivering the kind of care that you want for your patients. Good service means great "door to doc" times; good quality means not waiting to see the doc if you have a kidney stone, belly pain, or any other condition that could deteriorate. Good service means being informed about care; good quality means having information to make decisions about your care. Good service is adequate pain management; good quality is adequate pain management.

In the ED, service and quality are interwoven. The stress that a patient feels when he has to access the ED is noted in his vital signs. That stress is lessened when his environment is not harsh and unfeeling. There are excellent studies from the medical community that note that children do better when compassion and touch comes along with their care.

The emergency department is also the front door to the hospital. It gives patients their first impression of the hospital, and many of these patients go on to fill inpatient beds.

Do not consider this new attitude "consumerism," but think of it as going back to the roots of health care.

87.

How can we better manage patients' perception of wait time in the emergency department (ED)?

Question

Sometimes, once the decision has been made to admit the patient to an inpatient bed, there is not a bed available. It can take hours to get the patient to the unit. Some nurses find it difficult to continue to tell the patient the bed is not yet ready, so they avoid going in to talk with the patient/family. Do you have suggestions for how to best manage wait time in the ED, specific to key words for nurses to use?

Answer

Holding patients in the ED is no longer the exception, but a common practice. In the ED, we sometimes avoid communication with our patients at a time when communication is most needed.

As one CEO shared with me, it really is amazing what patients will forgive you for if you just explain, explain, explain. Tell them why the lab results are taking so long. Explain that it takes time for the media infusion to be absorbed before taking a CT scan, etc. When employees introduce themselves, make eye contact, smile, and explain, patients will even forgive you for a five-hour wait in the ED.

Some other ideas: consider setting a standard for how often someone checks on the patients who are waiting to be admitted. Every 30 minutes or every hour would be a good goal. Have RNs chart these communications so that you can verify.

Your desire for key words in this situation is warranted, so that all patients will hear the same message from staff. Use the wording from your patient satisfaction tool to craft key words that let the patients know that you care about them and that they are not an inconvenience. Also, use these key words to manage up the unit a given patient is being moved to.

Consider something like, "I just wanted to check on you to make sure you don't need anything while you wait to go upstairs. The nurses on six south are so wonderful; they will make sure you get very good care!" Or consider, "I am sorry your bed is not ready yet, but can I do something for you while you wait? I know the nurses in the CCU are working so hard to get a bed for you—they are just great!"

I worked with one ED that often held patients for days and instead of making the patients feel unwelcome and a burden, they would smile and tell the patients, "We like you so much we are keeping you another day!"

88. How can I get buy in for bedside registration in the emergency department (ED)?

Question

Let me first say my staff is great! I just cannot seem to get the buy in on bedside registration in the ED. Thanks for any suggestions you may have.

Answer

First, ask the ED Satisfaction Team or the nursing staff who do not see value in bedside registration to "secret shop." Have them be patients and walk your front-end process and see how many times they must stand and sit before they get to an ED bed. Without bedside registration this is sometimes five to seven times!

Second, if an ED staff doesn't move patients in a timely fashion, a "log jam" develops, which creates crisis. What is your door-to-bed time or your door-to-doc time? Measure this and estimate how much time you could cut off by doing bedside registration.

By doing bedside registration, and potentially cutting 10-20 minutes from your treat and release turnaround time for each patient, you have gained additional bed time and created virtual space. You probably already do bedside registration for ambulance patients, and it is an easy step to expand to all patients.

Third, you might try bedside registration with one individual or one shift before moving it to the entire department.

And finally, I would ask you if you are doing full registration before a medical screening exam is done. Remember, a medical screen determines if an emergency medical condition exists, and under EMTALA, insurance information is not requested until after this is done. Most EDs do not see bedside registration as a choice, but a necessity in complying with EMTALA regulations.

141

89.

How can a support department like human resources improve its score?

Question

We completed an internal survey targeting those areas that support staff in taking care of patients. One area that scored particularly low was human resources. They were concerned when they saw a mean score in the 40s related to accuracy and in the 50s related to timeliness. They very much want to improve but don't know where to start.

Answer

It's important to remember that scores can be low at first because this is the first time people have been asked for their feedback. Your hospital is making a positive move to improve health care and make a difference. I recommend having human resources focus on the positive responses they received in order to get buy in from the HR staff. Together with the HR Team, go through the survey and identify areas that moved from *good* to *very good* if you have previous results. Or, if it's the first time, look at who gave you high marks. This will help gain their confidence and inspire them to keep going. Then, focus on one or two poor responses that the staff feels are important to tackle. Ask managers of these areas to identify focus points to improve service. Create expectations with those managers that you can bring back to your staff, reach agreement on, and use in your rounding and communication.

Holding an expectation meeting early with each area you serve is a must to set a platform for success. Ask the leader to identify what your service would look like if he were very satisfied, building off of his feedback on the survey. You can then set expectations on a reasonable time frame and identify areas where you need the leader's assistance.

90.

How can we improve response to call lights?

Question

I am co-leader of the Inpatient/Outpatient Team. What is the best way to implement call light responses and improve response time?

Answer

Responding well to call lights is an important quality and risk issue. The best process focuses on eliminating call lights from going off in the first place. Most call lights are for toileting and positioning requests, pain medication requests, and personal needs requests. These reasons account for about 95 percent of call lights. The rest are urgent or emergent needs related to a patient's condition. By addressing the needs of patients in advance of the use of the call light, you improve response to those that do occur, because at that point you know to "drop and run." At the same time you save the staff work because there are fewer interruptions.

To accomplish this:
Do hourly rounds on the patient that focus on eliciting her needs prior to her asking via call light (typically shared by RNs and CNAs). Nurses put PRN pain medication on their list of scheduled things to do so that the patient does not have to use the call light to request them. Respond to IV pump alarms and cardiac/respiratory monitor alarms urgently.

In the process of hourly rounds, first accomplish the task you were scheduled to do for the patient. Then say to her, "Is there anything else I can do for you...I have time."

Once the patient says she's fine, do an environmental assessment of the room (call light, telephone, and TV control within reach, bedside table next to the bed, garbage can near bed, etc.). Then tell the patient, "Mrs. Johnson, I will be back to check on you in about an hour." By telling the patient when you will return, you give her the information to hold her next request until you come back. Patients will do this as long as the need isn't urgent or emergent.

Certainly any staff member should address a call light and can be trained to triage those requests. It becomes simpler if the above process is in place first. Call lights should be an "all hands on deck" activity.

91.

How can staff better manage multiple patient requests?

Question

I have been challenged to develop a top 10 list of appropriate responses to a patient's request that a nurse can use when she is too busy or working with a more critical patient. We have heard many examples of what not to say, and have offended patients when the nurses are trying to prioritize the patients' needs and requests. Your thoughts?

Answer

You probably have some nurse leaders who already do a good job with this. Pull your best nurse leaders and nurses together and ask them how they handle this issue. My feeling is they will give you what you are looking for and will feel good about coming up with the answer.

I also feel that nurses can work as a team, so that if one nurse is tied up with a critical patient and cannot meet routine requests from his other patients, another member of the team that day (charge nurse, staff nurse, or even the house supervisor) should step in to help. It's important that a critical patient be invisible to the rest of the patients so their care does not suffer as a result of that situation. Patients don't want their needs to be prioritized by someone else. They know only what is important to them.

The new nurse could say, "Your nurse is delayed with another patient, but is thinking of you and asked me to give you your pain medication (or whatever the request is). Your nurse, Jane, is committed to providing you with very good care and wants to make sure we are managing your pain even though she is tied up at the moment. Please let me know if there is anything else I can do for you until she's available. I have the time." This way, seamless care is provided regardless of short-term events. That defines quality.

I would also use a dual approach in that, during rounding, nurse leaders look for issues that are taking up too much nursing time and should be corrected.

These issues usually come under the area of tools and equipment, sub-par coworkers, systems that don't work well, and support department issues. Ask nursing staff how much time they would gain if the identified areas were fixed.

Finally, take a hard look at call lights and pain management. If these two areas are addressed, staff will have more time.

92. How can we increase patient satisfaction for meal service in hospitals?

Question

We would like some ideas about how to achieve 90th percentile patient satisfaction for meals while maintaining a productivity benchmark of 25 percent.

Answer

First, it is definitely possible to achieve above the 90th percentile in patient satisfaction while maintaining a productivity benchmark of 25 percent. We were able to achieve this at the last two hospitals in which I worked.

Here are some specific tips on how to improve food services' patient satisfaction scores:

- Begin with the meal options. Is there a good variety? How are meal options explained to patients? If a patient has a special meal plan ordered by her doctor, what information is available to help her understand her meal options and how they work for her? For each of the above, consider how information is shared with the patient. Is it in writing? When the meal options are selected, is anyone available to answer her questions prior to turning them in? Could the process be managed up better? Best practices include using "room service" selections versus limited meal options. When food services comes by to pick up the meal selection, they can ask the patient if she has any questions about her meal options.

- Next is delivery. When do meals show up at each floor? Review the timing of delivery. Round on each floor and ask nurses what feedback they have about the timing of meal services. Also ask if the food arrives at the proper temperature. Nurses are often the first to know how a patient feels about her meal service.

- Presentation and service. How is the food presented to the patient? Develop key words and key actions around the presentation and delivery. We call this the five fundamentals of service (Acknowledge, Introduce, Describe, Explain, Thank you). You can learn more about AIDET at www.studergroup.com. Just search on "five fundamentals."

Here is an example with respect to food service: 1. Knock on the door and ask permission to enter. **Acknowledge** the patient by name. 2. **Introduce** yourself by your first name and department and state why you are there. 3. **Describe.** Ask the patient where she would like her meal placed. Set it on her table, as appropriate. Show her the meal and reference how it was ordered to ensure you are delivering the correct meal. 4. **Explain.** Ask the patient if you can assist her with getting the meal within reach. Offer to help her open anything (milk carton, lids, etc.). Provide her with a card that explains her special meal plan (if appropriate). Consider using a tray liner that includes your goal to provide "very good" service and offer a number for her to call if she has any concerns or questions. 5. Finally, **thank the patient.** End by asking: "Is there anything else I can do for you?"

- Hardwire the five fundamentals of service as described above. One of the best methods is for you or your managers to round with staff members when they are picking up or delivering the meals. Use a log that tracks each person's performance: did he use all of the five fundamentals? Share these results with your staff members immediately.
- Round regularly on each patient floor. Ask nurses and patients key questions that relate specifically to your patient satisfaction questions. Use your rounding log to capture the information you receive, track follow-up, and find trends.

93. What makes a good waiting room experience?

Question

What are the essentials of a great waiting room experience in an outpatient setting?

Answer

We believe these actions are essential to a great waiting room experience and so we call them the five fundamentals of service:

1. Acknowledge patient by name.
2. Introduce yourself.
3. Describe. Let the patient know how to make himself comfortable, and explain who will be calling for him.
4. Explain delays so the patient understands why he must wait.
5. Thank the patient for coming.

In addition, seek any questions the patient may have. Collecting them up front is a big win and saves time. Also, remember to update the patient every 15 minutes if there is a delay, explaining why and how much longer. You may also want to call the area the "patient reception area" to reduce focus on wait. Having refreshments available can make a big difference and is usually more important than having a television.

The last component is a pre-call. It reduces anxiety and helps the patient arrive well prepared for the clinical experience.

94.

How can we raise our food temperature satisfaction?

Question

Our scores for food temperatures have been in the mid 80s. Do you know of other organizations that have improved their scores? Do you have pointers in how we can script our staff so that if patients aren't satisfied with their meal, they won't hesitate to let us know?

Answer

Here are some suggestions from a partner hospital in Florida:

- Put routine checkpoints in place that verify proper meal temperatures before the meal is ever brought to the unit for service. Depending upon the operational systems, this could be at the tray line or re-therm point.

- Evaluate travel time from the initial temperature checkpoint. It's common for meal temperatures to vary out of range if travel distance, elevator wait time, or other delays are not addressed.

- Ensure that the person who delivers the meal touches the plate lid or container just prior to entering the patient's room to verify that temperatures are within range.

- If a patient is asleep or out of the room for a test, avoid leaving the meal tray at the bedside table. Ideally, the tray should be placed in the unit's refrigerator and heated when the patient is ready to eat.

- Implement a check-back process that confirms the patient is pleased, not only with the meal temperature, but also with selection and quality in general.

Can you help us improve our cleanliness scores on our patient satisfaction survey?

Question

We are confused. We have very good scores on cleanliness in our inpatient areas, but have been unable to move the needle in our outpatient areas. What can we do?

Answer

First, review the scores in all outpatient areas (lab, waiting areas, mammography, radiology, etc.) and find out specifically what areas are perceived by the patient as not being cleaned to the highest level. Also, interview the supervisors in each outpatient area to see if their perceptions are consistent with patient indications on the survey. Check to see what departments have scores that are "satisfied" versus "very satisfied."

In training housekeeping staff, I would provide AIDET training on the five fundamentals. (Visit www.studergroup.com and search on "five fundamentals.") This will increase staff visibility to the patients and their families. Having staff say "good morning" and "good afternoon" can have a positive impact on patient and family perception.

The last tip is to post a "cleaned with care" card that is signed by the EVS employee, along with the date. This should be placed in public view (i.e., on an end table).

96.

Is writing an apology appropriate for service recovery?

Question

We would like to print cards with our logo and some phrase/mission/value statement to be used for patient service recovery. One program we are looking at is writing a personal note to the patient when we have failed to apologize and explain how the situation is being addressed. Does this make sense?

Answer

I think your idea to use the hospital's logo and mission is excellent. The message needs to be written by hand. My suggestion for effective service recovery is that you include 1) a thank you to the patient for bringing this issue to your attention; 2) an apology: *We are sorry you did not receive the care you were expecting*; 3) a request for input: *We want to fix this, and if you have any ideas on how we can improve this, please provide them.*

When it is too late to repair the problem, ask what you can do to repair the relationship. My experience is that 99 percent of the time, the patient will say, "I just don't want it to happen to anyone else." Follow up with a note telling the patient that this won't happen again because you have fixed the problem by _____ _____(describe changes you've made). Thank the patient for helping you to provide better care.

Two final points:
1. Let the patient know to contact you if he ever needs health care again, so you can assist him in obtaining the best care.
2. Flag him in the system, so you are aware he's had a problem and can greet him the next time he visits.

CHAPTER 7

HOW CAN I IMPROVE PHYSICIAN RELATIONSHIPS?

Satisfied physicians are as important to a great hospital as satisfied employees and satisfied patients. Leaders play a critical role in ensuring the five main physician satisfiers are hardwired: quality, efficiency, input, appreciation, and telling the truth!

97.

What are the drivers for physician satisfaction?

Question

What are the drivers for physician satisfaction in the hospital setting?

Answer

The key drivers are *quality, efficiency, input, appreciation,* and *telling the truth.* Specifically, physicians want the following:

- Quality: Assurance that their patients are receiving quality care.
- Efficient Operations: Lab results should be on charts when physicians do their rounding, operating rooms should start on time, nurses should have charts when they call physicians, transcriptions should be turned around quickly, and staff should be retained.
- Input: When running small focus groups of physicians I have asked: "For you to feel great about practicing medicine at this hospital—and to feel that patients are receiving great care—what would our service to you and your patients look like?" I then worked with them to rank their suggestions in order of importance. I picked one I could impact, focused on it, and then communicated the results over and over.
- Appreciation: Say thank you. Recently a person told one of our Studer Group Coaches that she heard me speak, and though she wanted to believe, she was skeptical. However, she took action anyway. She wrote a note to a physician thanking him for the patient care he provides, and then commented that his family must be so supportive of him. Some weeks later, at a community event, the physician's wife came up to her to say how much her note had impacted her husband. The physician's

wife started to cry, saying that no one had ever thanked her for what she does to support her husband. Point one: physicians appreciate being appreciated. Point two: practice the behavior of recognizing physicians and focus on the positive. Point three: understanding sometimes follows action.

- Tell the truth. If you can't meet a physician's needs, explain why. Similarly, visibility, availability, and accessibility are also key drivers for physician satisfaction.

Key Discouragements for Physicians:
1. Lack of input and follow-through.
2. Inefficiency.
3. Lack of proactive behavior. Once, I was at a Los Angeles hospital whose surgery nurse leader is phenomenal. Since she has arrived, they have not needed agency or registry staff, volume is up, and on time starts have significantly improved. She also put in a system that if the OR is running behind, physicians are updated consistently so they do not have to wait.
4. Lack of appreciation for their time and skill.
5. Vagueness. Say *yes, no,* or when you will have a yes or no.

98.

What can I do about disruptive physician conduct?

Question

Disruptive physician conduct has become a concern at our facility. Have you encountered any methods or practices that have proven successful regarding this issue?

Answer

I have several suggestions:

- Involve physicians on the Service Teams where appropriate.
- Ask physicians to model behavior consistent with your organization's standards of behavior and sign a written copy detailing the standards as employees do.
- Recognize those physicians who model expected behavior, thus making it more uncomfortable for those who don't. Also, the chief of staff must make some hard decisions regarding appropriate sanctioning of physicians.
- If you have a policy to sanction physicians for medical record policies, consider doing the same with standards of performance and core values.
- If your organization uses 360 peer reviews, solicit input from staff for 360s for physicians. The topics rated on the nurse/staff survey include: treats staff with respect and collegial attitude; documents in a timely fashion and compliant with department policies; gives staff proper notice for project completion; recognizes staff efforts; resolves conflicts in a private setting and with confidentiality; arrives on time to OR, practice site; responsive to staff needs/requests; communicates plan of care

clearly; educates staff re: new treatment, equipment, and so forth.

When an organization asks a disruptive physician to leave, you know it is committed to change. But it's equally important to recognize the other 90 percent or more of physicians who are very supportive of the journey from good to great.

For more information, read my article titled "Getting Physicians on Board" at www.studergroup.com.

How can we make nursing phone calls to physicians more effective?

Question

Some of our physicians complain that when RNs or clinicians call for change of meds, review test results, etc., the caller does *not* have all the pertinent info about the patient. Physicians are then put on hold, which frustrates them immensely. Is there a checklist that an RN/clinician can use *before* picking up the phone?

Answer

I agree with physicians. A number of hospitals have created checklists and key words to address and resolve this issue.

For example, one organization has developed a "Calling Docs Card" that is displayed in nurses' stations. It includes a checklist of tasks to be completed before calling on a physician. Another created a flier that simply says, "Got Chart?" with a list of reminders that all nurses or clinicians can review prior to calling on their physicians.

You can place the card or "Got Chart?" flier at all nurses' stations by phones. Make sure all staff have completed items on the checklist before calling on physicians. You can download both these tools at www.studergroup.com. Search on "physician satisfiers."

100.

Should we have a Physician Satisfaction Team?

Question

If we are supposed to buy into the idea that we can all make a difference, and that we are all in it together, then why do we have a separate team for doctors?

Answer

Yes, there is a separate team for employees, but the reality is the physician is an independent member of the medical staff. Physicians partner with caregivers to provide care. Therefore, they are customers to the hospital. I see the existence of the Physician Satisfaction Team in terms of providing quality and efficiency to physicians so we can provide better care to patients. That's really what it's all about.

101.

Can I apply your principles to my surgical group?

Question

I am a member of a surgical group and would very much like to take some of these principles into my office. Has anyone attempted this? If so, I'd like a little guidance.

Answer

Yes, we have seen physicians take these principles into their offices with excellent results. In the span of two years, one medical group increased patient satisfaction from the 37th percentile to the 85th, moved employee satisfaction above the 90th percentile, and had physician turnover at less than 2 percent with physician satisfaction in the 90th percentile.

The key steps they took:
Constant Measuring—Every week the receptionist gave out five surveys for each physician, using a medical group survey tool. Results from three questions, including overall manner of the physician and overall quality of care of visit, were tabulated and shared with individual physicians and leaders on a bimonthly basis.

Rounding—The physician leader and office manager hardwired rounding on staff and other physicians and coordinated their rounding for alignment.

Leadership Development—Key physicians attended training that looked at leadership skill sets such as communication and dealing with difficult patients to give them tools to be successful.

Implemented thank you notes, key words, and post-visit calls for new patients.

Tied physician compensation and leader evaluations to measurable results.

Bright Ideas Program

A program whereby employees are encouraged to submit quality ideas on an ongoing basis that help make the organization a better place for employees to work, physicians to practice, and patients to receive care. Bright ideas offer organizations a way to drive individual accountability, foster a culture of ownership, drive innovation, and impact the bottom line.

Burning Platform

The issue or set of issues (e.g., cost of high employee turnover, stagnant patient satisfaction, survival of the organization) that creates a sense of urgency organizationwide to use new tools and behaviors to realize gains in Service and Operational Excellence.

Connecting the Dots

Using key words to link actions to the goals and values of the organization and help others understand what you are doing and why. This can be done throughout all activities (i.e., awards, announcements, thank you's, staff meetings, new policies, etc.).

DESK Approach

An approach to follow when meeting with low performing employees. D—Describe what has been observed; E—Evaluate how you feel; S—Show what needs to be done; K—Know consequences of continued same performance.

Employee Forums

Quarterly meetings led by senior leaders to communicate a consistent message to all employees about progress and results and to celebrate and recognize achievements. Employee forums occur at set intervals with a predetermined agenda that is tied to the Five Pillars (People, Service, Quality, Finance, and Growth). Leaders set the expectation that all employees must attend.

Five Fundamentals of Service

The five fundamentals of service (or AIDET) that, when used together, ensure excellent patient satisfaction. A—Acknowledge the patient; I—Introduce yourself, your skill set, your professional certification, and your training; D—Duration of the test/exam; E—Explanation of the test and what happens next; T—Thank the patient for choosing your hospital.

Hardwire

The process by which an organization, department, team, or individual integrates a behavior or action into the daily operations.

Harvest Wins

The action of taking positive information learned and sharing it with others. This action will not only help people feel they have purpose, do worthwhile work, and make a difference, but also allow others to learn from others' success. Behavior that is rewarded and recognized will be repeated.

Healthcare Flywheel^{SM}

A teaching tool/diagram that illustrates the power that purpose, passion, to do's, and results have in creating momentum in an organization. Studer Group developed the Healthcare Flywheel to help organizations understand the journey in creating great places for employees to work, physicians to practice, and patients to receive care.

Key Words at Key Times

Things said and done to "connect the dots" and help patients, families, and visitors better understand what we are doing. They align our words with our actions to give a consistent experience and message.

Leadership Development Institutes (LDIs)

Off-site leadership training self-sponsored by the organization. Leaders participate in two-day LDIs every 90 days to develop focused skills to achieve organizational goals, improve and standardize leadership performance, and ensure organizational consistency. An organization's goals under the Five Pillars guide the framework for establishing the objectives and curriculum for each of the LDI sessions.

Manage Up

A form of communication that positions physicians, colleagues, and supervisors positively to others in the organization and to patients (e.g., using reward, recognition, and introducing clinician skill sets to patients).

Must Haves^{SM}

Best practices identified and used at high-performing organizations in Studer Group's national learning lab. Based on Studer Group's Nine Principles®, these actions and "to do's" include: (1) Rounding for Outcomes, (2) Employee Thank You Notes, (3) Selection and the First 90 Days, (4) Discharge Phone Calls, (5) Key Words at Key Times, and (6) Aligning Leader Evaluations with Desired Behaviors.

Nine Principles®

A sequenced, step-by-step process and road map to attain desired results and help leaders develop and achieve an excellence-based culture. The Nine Principles are (1) Commit to Excellence, (2) Measure the Important Things, (3) Build a Culture Around Service, (4) Create and Develop Leaders, (5) Focus on Employee Satisfaction, (6) Build Individual Accountability, (7) Align Behavior with Goals and Values, (8) Communicate at All Levels, and (9) Reward and Recognize Success.

Pillars

A foundation and framework used to set organizational goals and the evaluation process. Once the goals for each Pillar are set for the organization as a whole, they are cascaded throughout, from the division level to department or unit level to individual leader. Most organizations use the Five Pillars: People, Service, Quality, Finance, and Growth. These can be customized to fit specific language or organizational terms, or other Pillars can be added, such as Community. These Pillars then lay the framework for consistent evaluations, communications, and work planning.

Prescriptive To Do's

Techniques, tools, and behaviors that will achieve results under goals that organizations set under the Five Pillars. These guiding principles help leaders focus on how to implement actions that will have the greatest impact and provide a step-by-step road map to getting and sustaining results.

Pushback

Resistance received from employees, physicians, and leadership.

Rounding for Outcomes

The consistent practice of asking specific questions of key stakeholders—leaders, employees, physicians, and patients—to obtain actionable information. Includes unit leader rounding, senior leader rounding, support service rounding, and rounding on patients.

Accelerate the momentum of your Healthcare Flywheel^{SM}. Access these resources at www.studergroup.com . . .

1. Read articles and download tools.

Learn more with free access to:

- **Articles**—A collection of short articles written by Studer Group authors available via email. Read about, for example, *Reducing Leadership Variance, Why Some Organizations Get Results Faster Than Others, It's Patient Perception of Care—Not a Number*, and *Building a Mature Leadership Team*.
- **Ask Quint and Studer Group Coaches**—Read dozens of the most recent answers to questions like the ones in this book.
- **Tools**—Information you can use right away to effect change. Download a rounding log, a thank you note grid, tools to prepare for JCAHO readiness, and others referenced in this book.

2. Order *Hardwiring Excellence.*

Since its publication in April 2004, thousands of leaders have read Quint Studer's first book for an in-depth understanding of how Studer Group's Nine Principles® create and sustain service and operational excellence. To accelerate cultural change in your organization, order copies for board members and senior leaders first. Then share copies with all staff.

3. Attend Studer Group Institutes.

Choose from *Taking You and Your Organization to the Next Level*, presented by Quint Studer, *The Nuts and Bolts of Service Excellence in the Emergency Department*, and *Focusing Nine Principles® on Food and Environmental Service*. Look for a calendar of upcoming events on the Studer Group homepage.

4. Attend Studer Group's "What's Right in Health Care" Conference.

Studer Group's annual two-day conference features presentations on service and operational excellence by leaders at health care organizations nationwide. Attendees take home prescriptive solutions and a renewed passion for making a difference.

5. Learn about the Must Haves℠ videos.

This outcome-based train-the-trainer series hardwires the Must Haves: Rounding for Outcomes, Employee Thank You Notes, Selection and the First 90 Days, Discharge Phone Calls, and Key Words at Key Times. Jointly produced by Studer Group and the Cleveland Clinic Foundation, the videos are available individually or in a set.

6. Read *Hardwired Results*, Studer Group's quarterly magazine.

Focused around a unique theme (e.g., employee loyalty, engaged leadership), each issue offers tools, tips, and techniques to create and sustain service and operational excellence. Organizational case studies from Studer Group's national learning lab support learning.

7. Watch *Moving Organizational Performance: HighMiddleLow^SM Performer Conversations*.

The management techniques featured in this two-part video have been identified by hospitals in Studer Group's national learning lab as prime building blocks for creating and sustaining excellence. Train leaders to re-recruit high performers, develop skills in middle performers, and confront low performers with required steps for improvement.

8. Use *Leader Evaluation Manager^SM, Results through Accountability*.

Leader Evaluation Manager software automates the Studer Group accountability process through leader evaluations, monthly report cards, and 90-Day Plans to chart a clear path from action to results. The weighted goals across the Pillars and objective rating scale further drive performance. Leaders can enter, access, and share goals and data efficiently.

9. Listen to the audio seminar "Tools for Leaders: Rounding."

Available on CD-ROM. Quint Studer shares insights and best practices on Rounding for Outcomes.

10. Determine keynote availability.

Contact Studer Group at (850) 934-1099 to identify a keynote presenter and topic to meet the specific needs of your organization or event. Quint Studer and Studer Group Coaches frequently present on hardwiring excellence, the Nine Principles® of Service and Operational Excellence, and offer a wide range of customized topics geared to leaders, physicians, employees, and industry groups.